MW01200353

Strange News
from
Another Star

Hermann Hesse

Strange News from Another Star
Merkwürdige Nachricht von einem anderen Stern
Written in April 1915
First Published in "Märchen" in 1919
by
S. Fischer Verlag
Copyright © 1919 S. Fischer Verlag

This translation copyright © 2014 by Clyve Parker Communications
Cover design by Jen Davis

First Edition

AN: 9 8 7 6 5 4 3 2 1

Copyright © 2014 Pygmaion LLP
All rights reserved.
ISBN-10: 1500348813
ISBN-13: 978-1500348816

Contents

Strange News from Another Star

In a southern province of our beautiful planet a terrible catastrophe occurred. A violent earthquake followed by thunder storms and floods destroyed three large villages with their fields, gardens, forests and farms.

Many people died. However, the saddest thing of all was that the villagers ran out of flowers and could not make enough funeral bouquets to adorn the graves of their dead relatives.

Immediately after the horrible storms subsided, those who remained alive took care of everything that needed to be done and messengers were dispatched to neighboring towns with pleas for aid and charity.

From all the towers of the entire province, chanters could be heard singing salutation to the Goddess of compassion, stirring and deeply touching verses known for ages to move all those who listen to offer help and assistance. From all the towns and cities, large groups of rescuers and helpers answered the call. Food, clothes, wagons, horses, tools, stones, wood, and many other useful things were brought from all neighboring regions.

The injured were carefully washed and bandaged. The old men, women, and children were comforted, consoled, and led away to shelters by kindly hands. Those unfortunate enough to lose the roofs over their heads were overwhelmed by kind invitations and managed to take refuge in the homes of relatives, friends, and strangers.

While some people searched for quake victims under the ruins, others began to clear away the fallen roofs, to prop up the unstable walls with beams, and to prepare for the quick reconstruction of the villages. There was a cloud of horror hanging in the air with the many dead reminding everyone that this was a time of mourning and austere silence.

Yet a sober readiness and a certain vibrant mood could be detected on the faces and in the voices of people. It was as if they were inspired by their common action and zeal and the certainty that they were doing something unusual and necessary, something commendable and deserving of thanks.

Initially people had worked in silence and awe, but cheerful voices and the soft sounds of singing could soon be heard here and there. Two ancient songs were among the favorites that were sung: "Blessed are those who bring help to those in need; they drink good deeds like thirsty gardens drink the first rainfall and respond with flowers of gratitude." and "The serenity of God flows from common action."

The first dead bodies to be found were buried and adorned with flowers and branches gathered from the destroyed gardens. However, when they discovered that they did not have enough flowers for all the burials, people began fetching flowers from neighboring villages.

The three destroyed villages were the ones with the largest and most beautiful gardens of flowers during this time of year. It was there that visitors came each year to see the narcissus and irises because they could not be found anywhere else in such big quantities. The flowers were always cultivated with great care and had remarkably different colors. But all this was now devastated and ruined.

The people were perplexed. They did not know how

to follow the customary rites regarding the burial of the dead. Tradition required that before burial each human and each animal get adorned lavishly with flowers of the season. The burial ritual was always richer and more impressive when death was sudden and more sorrowful.

The elder Chief of the province, who was one of the first to appear with help in his wagon, found himself so overwhelmed by questions, requests, and complaints that he had difficulty keeping his composure. However, he took heart and his eyes remained bright and friendly and his voice remained clear and polite. Through his white beard, his lips maintained a silent and kind smile that suited him as the wise counselor of the province.

"Friends," he said, "a calamity has struck us. It was most likely sent by the gods to test us. Whatever has been destroyed here, we shall rebuild for our brothers and give it all back to them. I thank the gods that I've been able to experience in my old age how all of you managed to stop whatever you were doing and came here to help.

But where are we going to find the flowers to adorn all the dead? How are we going to celebrate their transformation in a beautiful and reverent manner? As long as we are alive and well, we must make sure that not a single one of those weary pilgrims be buried without their rightful floral tribute. Do you all agree?"

"Yes," they replied. "We all agree."

"I knew it," said the Chief elder in his fatherly voice. "Now I want to tell you, my friends, what we must do. We must carry all the remains that cannot be buried today to the large summer temple high in the mountains, where snow is still on the ground.

They will be safe there and will not decompose before we bring them flowers. Only one person can really help us obtain so many flowers at this time of the year, and that is the King. We must send one of us to the King to request his assistance."

Again all the people nodded and cried out, "Yes, yes, to the King!"

"So be it," the Chief elder continued, and everyone was pleased to see his pleasant smile glistening from beneath his white beard.

"But whom shall we send to the King? He must be young and robust because he shall travel far on our best horse. He must be handsome and kind and have sparkling eyes, so the King's heart will not be able to resist him. He needn't say much, but his eyes must be able to speak. Clearly, it would be best if we sent a child, the handsomest child in the community. But how could he possibly undertake such a journey? Friends, you must help me. If there is anyone here who wants to volunteer to be the messenger, or if you know somebody suitable for this task, please tell me."

The Chief elder stopped and looked around with his bright eyes, but nobody stepped forward. Not a single voice could be heard. When he repeated the question a second, and then a third time, a young man suddenly emerged from the crowd.

He was sixteen years old, practically still a boy, and he fixed his eyes on the ground and blushed as he greeted the elder Chief.

As soon as the Chief looked at him, he realized the young man was the perfect messenger. So he smiled and said, "It's wonderful that you want to be our messenger. But why is it that, among all those people, you should be the one to volunteer?"

The young man raised his eyes to the old man and said, "If there is no one else who wants to volunteer, then I should be the one to go."

Someone from the crowd shouted, "Send him,

Chief. We know him. He comes from our village, and the earthquake destroyed his flower garden. It was the most beautiful in the region."

The Chief gave the young man a friendly look and asked, "Are you sad about what happened to your flowers?"

The young man responded softly, "Yes, I'm sorry, but that is not why I volunteered. I had a dear friend and also a splendid young horse, both were killed by the earthquake. Now they are lying in our yard and we must have flowers so that they can be buried."

The Chief placed his hands on the young man's head and blessed him and the villagers brought him one of their best horses.

The young man jumped onto the horse's back, nodded farewell to the people, slapped the horse on the neck, dashed out of the village and headed straight across the wet and ravaged fields.

He rode the entire day, and in order to reach the distant capital and see the King as soon as he could, he ventured over mountainous terrain. As it got dark and the shades of evening fell, he led his horse by the reins up a steep path through the forest and rocks.

A large dark bird, a kind that he had never seen before, flew ahead of him. The young man followed the bird until it landed on the roof of a small open temple. He left his horse and walked through wooden pillars into the temple's sanctuary. There he found a sacrificial altar. It was a simple solid block made of a black stone not usually found in that region.

An obscure symbol of a deity, that the messenger did not recognize, was carved on the stone. It had the shape of man whose heart was being devoured by a vulture.

The young man paid tribute to the deity by offering a bluebell flower that he had plucked at the foot of the mountain and stuck in the lapel of his coat. He then lay down in a corner of the temple.

He was very tired and needed to sleep. But he could not fall asleep as easily as he was accustomed to at home each evening. Perhaps it was the bluebell on the stone, or something else. Whatever it was, something odd disturbed him by exuding a penetrating and scintillating aroma. The eerie symbol of the god glimmered like a ghost in the dark hall and the strange bird sat on the roof and vigorously flapped its gigantic wings from time to time. It seemed as if a storm were brewing.

In the middle of the night, the young man got up, went outside the temple, and looked up at the bird. The bird raised and lowered its wings, then asked "Why aren't you sleeping?"

"I don't know," the young man replied. "Perhaps it's because I've suffered."

"What exactly have you suffered?"

"My friend and my favorite horse were both killed in a quake."

"Is dying so bad?" the bird asked disdainfully.

"Oh, no, it's not so bad. It's only a farewell. But that's not the reason why I'm sad. It is because we cannot bury my friend and my splendid horse. We have no more flowers to adorn them."

"There are worse things than that," said the bird, ruffling its feathers indignantly.

"No, there is certainly nothing worse than this. Whoever is buried without a floral tribute cannot be reborn the way his heart desires. Whoever buries his dead people without a floral tribute continues to see their shadows in his dreams. You see, I already can't sleep because my dead people are without flowers."

The bird rasped and screeched with its bent beak, "Young boy, you know nothing about suffering if this is all you've experienced. Haven't you ever heard about the great evils? About hatred, murder, and jealousy?"

As he listened to these words, the young man thought he was dreaming. Then he collected himself and said discreetly, "Yes, bird, I can remember. These things are written in the old stories and tales. But they have nothing to do with reality. Perhaps it was that way once upon a time in the world. Before there were flowers and gods that are good. Who in the world still thinks about such things as that now?"

The bird laughed softly with its raspy voice. Then it stretched itself taller and said to the young man, "And now you want to go to the King, and I'm to show you the way?"

"Oh, you already know!" the young man joyfully exclaimed. "Yes I'd appreciate it if you'd lead me there."

The great bird floated silently to the ground, spread out its wings without making a sound, and asked the young man to leave his horse behind and fly with him to the King. The messenger climbed up to the bird's back and prepared himself for the ride.

"Close your eyes," the bird commanded, and the young man did as he was told. They flew softly and silently through the dark sky, like an owl. The messenger could hear only the cold wind whistling in his ears.

They flew and flew the entire night, when it was nearly morning they came to a stop and the bird cried out "Open your eyes!"

The young man opened his eyes and saw that he was standing on the edge of a forest. Beneath him was a plain that glistened so brightly in the early hours that its light almost blinded him.

"You'll find me here in the forest when you come back.", the bird said, then it shot into the sky like an

7

arrow and disappeared into the blue.

The young messenger began wandering from the forest into the broad plain when a strange feeling came over him. Everything around him was so different and changed that he did not know whether he was awake or dreaming.

Meadows and trees were just as they were at home. The sun shone, and the wind played in the fresh grass. But there were no people or animals, no houses or gardens to be seen. It seemed as if an earthquake had taken its toll here just as it did back in his home country. Ruins, broken branches, uprooted trees, wrecked fences, and lost farm equipment were spread all over the landscape.

He saw a dead man lying in the middle of a field. He had not been buried and was horribly decomposed. He felt a deep revulsion at the sight of the dead body. Nausea swelled up within him. He had never seen anything like it. The dead man's face was not covered and seemed to have been ravaged by vultures as it decayed. The young man gathered some green leaves and flowers and covered the dead man's face.

An inexpressible, disgusting, and stifling smell hung in the tepid air and seemed glued to the entire plain. The young man saw another corpse lying in the grass with ravens circling overhead.

There was a horse without its head and human bones scattered under the sun. There seemed to have been no thought of a floral tribute and burial.

He feared that an incredible catastrophe might have caused the death of every single person in this country. He feared that there were so many dead he would never be able to pick enough flowers to cover their faces.

Full of dread, with half-closed eyes, he wandered farther. The stench of decaying flesh and blood swept toward him from all sides. An even stronger wave of unspeakable misery and suffering rose from a thousand different piles of corpses and rubble.

The messenger thought that he was caught in an awful dream. Perhaps it was a warning from the divine powers because his own dead were still without their floral tribute and burial. He recalled what the mysterious bird told him the night before, on the temple roof, and heard its sharp voice once more claiming, "There are much worse things."

He realized that the bird might have carried him to another planet and that everything he saw was real and true. He remembered the feeling he used to experience when he, occasionally, listened to ghastly tales of primeval times. It was this same exact feeling he was experiencing now; a horrid chill.

Behind the chill, there was a quiet pleasant feeling of comfort, for all this was infinitely far away from him and had long since passed. Everything here seemed like a horror story. The whole strange world of atrocities, corpses, and vultures seemed to have no meaning or order. It seemed to follow some incomprehensible laws, insane laws, according to which bad, foolish, and nasty things occurred instead of beautiful and good things.

He noticed a live human being walking across the field, a farmer or a hired hand, and he ran quickly toward him, calling out. When the man approached, he was horrified, and his heart was overcome by compassion, for this farmer was terribly ugly and no longer resembled anything like a child of the sun.

He seemed more like a man accustomed to thinking only about himself and to seeing only false, ugly, and horrible things happen everywhere, like a man who lived constantly in ghastly nightmares.

There was not a trace of serenity or kindness in his

eyes and in his entire face and being, no gratitude or trust. This unfortunate creature seemed to be without the least trace of virtue. But the messenger pulled himself together and approached the man with great friendliness, as though the man was marked by misfortune. He greeted him in brotherly fashion and spoke to him with a smile.

The ugly man stood as though paralyzed, looking bewildered with his large, bleary eyes. His voice was rough and without music, like the growl of a primitive creature. However, it was impossible for the ugly man to resist the messenger's cheerful and trustworthy look.

After he had stared at the stranger for a while, the farmer expressed a kind of smile or grin on his rugged and crude face. Ugly, maybe, but gentle and astonished like the first little smile of a reborn soul that has just risen from the lowest region of the earth.

"What do you want from me?" the farmer asked the young stranger.

The young man responded according to the custom of his native country: "I thank you, friend, and I beg you to tell me whether I can be of service to you."

When the farmer did not reply but only stared and smiled with embarrassment, the messenger said to him, "Tell me, friend, what is going on here? What are all these horrible and terrible things?" And he pointed all around him.

The farmer had difficulty understanding him, and when the messenger repeated his question, the farmer said, "Haven't you ever seen this before? This is war. This is a battlefield."

The farmer pointed to a dark pile of ruins and said, "That was my house." And when the stranger looked into his murky eyes with deep sympathy, the farmer lowered them and looked down at the ground.

"Don't you have a king?" the young man asked, and when the farmer said yes, he asked further, "Where is he?"

The man pointed to a small, barely visible encampment in the distance. The messenger said farewell by placing his hand on the man's forehead, then departed. In response, the farmer felt his forehead with both hands, shook his heavy head with concern, and stared after the stranger for a long time.

The messenger walked and walked over rubble and past horrifying sights until he arrived at the encampment. Armed men were standing here and there or scurrying about.

Nobody seemed to notice him, and he walked between the people and the tents until he found the largest and most decorated tent, which belonged to the King. Once there, he entered.

The King was sitting on a simple low camp bed inside the tent. Next to him lay his coat and behind him, in deep shadow, crouched his servant, who had fallen asleep. The King sat bent over in deep thought. His face was handsome and sad; a crop of gray hair hung over his tanned forehead. His sword lay before him on the ground.

The young man greeted the King silently with sincere respect, just as he would have greeted his own King. He remained standing with his arms folded across his chest until the King glanced at him.

"Who are you?" the King asked severely, drawing his dark eyebrows together.

The King's glance fell on the pure and serene features of the stranger as the young man regarded him with trust and friendliness.

The King's voice grew milder. "I've seen you once before," he said, trying to recall. "You resemble somebody I knew in my childhood."

"I'm a stranger," said the messenger.

"Then it was a dream," remarked the King softly. "You remind me of my mother. Say something to me. Tell me why you are here."

The young man began: "A bird brought me here. There was an earthquake in my country. We want to bury our dead, but there are no flowers."

"No flowers?" said the King.

"No, no more flowers. It is terrible, isn't it, when people want to bury their dead and the floral tribute cannot be celebrated? After all, it's important for people to experience their transformation in glory and joy."

Suddenly it occurred to the messenger that there were many dead people on the horrible field who had not yet been buried, and he held his breath while the King regarded him, nodded, and sighed deeply.

"I wanted to seek out our King and request he send us more flowers," the messenger continued. "But as I was in the temple on the mountain, a great bird came and said he wanted to bring me to the King, and he carried me through the skies to you.

It was the roof of a temple of an unknown deity, where the bird sat. This god had a most peculiar symbol on his altar. His heart was being devoured by a vulture. During the night, I had a conversation with that great bird and it is only now that I understand its words. It said there is much more suffering and many more terrible things in the world than I knew.

And now I am here and have crossed the large field and have seen endless suffering and misfortune during this short time, much more than there is in our most horrible tales, I come to you, oh King, and would like to ask you if I can be of any service to you."

The King, who listened attentively, tried to smile but his handsome face was so serious and bitter and sad that he could not.

"I thank you." he said. "You've already been of service to me. You've reminded me of my mother and I thank you for this."

The young man was disturbed because the King could not smile. "You're so sad," he said. "Is it because of this war?"

"Yes," said the King.

The young man had the feeling that the King was a noble man who was deeply depressed, and he could not refrain from breaking a rule of courtesy and asking him a straightforward question: "Please tell me, why are you waging such wars on your planet? Who's to blame for all this? Are you yourself responsible?"

The King stared at the messenger for a long time. He seemed indignant and angry at the audacity of the question. However, he was not able to maintain his gloomy look as he peered into the bright and innocent eyes of the stranger.

"You're a child," said the King, "and there are things that you can't understand. War is nobody's fault. It occurs by itself, like thunder and lightning. All of us who must fight wars are not the perpetrators. We are all victims."

"Then you must all die very easily?" the young man asked. "In my country death is not at all feared, and most people go willingly to their death. Many approach their transformation with joy. But nobody would ever dare to kill another human being. It must be different on your planet."

"People are indeed killed here," said the King, shaking his head. "But we consider killing the worst of crimes. Only in war are people permitted to kill because nobody kills for his own advantage. Nobody kills out of hate or envy. Rather, they do what the society demands.

Still, you'd be mistaken to believe that my people die easily. You just have to look into the faces of our dead and you will see that they have difficulty dying. They die hard and unwillingly."

The young man listened to all this and was astounded by the sadness and gravity in the lives of the people on this planet.

He would have liked to ask many more questions, but he had a clear sense that he would never grasp the complex nature of all these obscure and terrible things. Indeed, he felt no great desire now to understand them.

Either these sorrowful people were creatures of an inferior order, or they had not been blessed by the light of the gods and were still ruled by demons. Perhaps a singular mishap was determining the course of life on this planet.

It seemed to him much too painful and cruel to keep questioning the King, compelling him to provide answers and make confessions that could only be bitter and humiliating for him. He was sorry for these people who lived in gloom and dread of death and nevertheless killed each other in droves. These people, whose faces took on shabby and crude expressions like that of the farmer, or who had expressions of deep and terrible sorrow like that of the King. They seemed to him to be rather peculiar, almost ridiculous, and foolish in a disturbing and shameful way.

There was one more question, however, that the young man could not repress. Even if these poor creatures were backward, children behind the times, children of a latter-day star without peace. Even if their lives ran their course as a convulsive cramp and ended in desperate slaughter. Even if they let their dead lie on the fields and perhaps even ate them, for horror tales were told about such things occurring in primitive times, they must still have a premonition of the future, a dream of the gods, some spark of soul in them. Otherwise this entire unpleasant world would be only a meaningless mistake.

"Forgive me, King," the young man said with a flattering voice. "Forgive me if I ask you one more question before I leave your strange country."

"Go ahead," replied the King, who was perplexed by this stranger, for the young man seemed to have a sensitive, mature, and insightful mind in many ways, but in others he seemed to be a small child whom one had to protect and was not to be taken seriously.

"My foreign King," spoke the messenger, "you've made me sad. You see, I've come from another country, and the great bird on the temple roof was right. There is infinitely more misery here than I could have imagined.

Your life seems to be a dreadful nightmare, and I don't know whether you are ruled by gods or demons. You see, King, we have a legend, I used to believe that it was all fairy tale rubbish and empty smoke.

It is a legend about how such things as war and death and despair were common in our country at one time. These terrible words, which we have long since stopped using in our language, can be read in collections of our old tales, and they sound awful to us and even a little ridiculous.

Today I've learned that these tales are all true and I see you, and your people, dying and suffering in that way which I've known only from the terrible legends of primeval times.

So now tell me, don't you have in your soul a sort of intimation that you're not doing the right thing? Don't you have a yearning for bright, serene gods, for sensible and cheerful leaders and mentors?

Don't you ever dream in your sleep about another,

more beautiful life where nobody is envious of others, where reason and order prevail, where people treat other people only with cheerfulness and consideration?

Don't you know anything about what we at home call music and divine worship and bliss?"

As he listened to these words, the King's head sank, and when he raised it again, his face had been transformed. It glowed radiantly with a smile, even though there were tears in his eyes.

"Beautiful boy," said the King, "I don't know for certain whether you're a child or a sage. But I can tell you that we sense all this and cradle it in our souls, all that you have mentioned. We have intimations of happiness, freedom, and gods. Indeed, we have a legend about a wise man who lived long ago and who perceived the unity of the worlds as harmonious music of the heavenly spheres. Does this answer suffice?

You see, you may be a blessed creature from another world, or you may even be a God. Whatever the case may be, you have no happiness in your heart, no power, no will that does not live as an intuition, a reflection, a distant shadow in our hearts, too."

Suddenly, the King stood up and the young man was surprised for the King's face was soaked, for a moment, in a bright clear smile like the first rays of the sun.

"Go now," he ordered the messenger. "Go, and let us fight and murder! You've made my heart soft. You've reminded me of my mother. Enough, enough of this, you dear handsome boy. Go now, and flee before the next battle begins!

I'll think of you when the blood flows and the cities burn, and I'll think of the world as a whole, and how our folly and fury and ruthlessness cannot separate us from it. Farewell, and give my regards to your planet, and give my regards to your deity, whose symbol is a heart being devoured by a vulture. I know this heart, and I know that vulture very well.

And don't forget, my handsome friend from a distant land: When you think of your friend, the poor King in war, do not think of him as he sat on a camp bed plunged in deep sorrow. Think of him with tears in his eyes and blood on his hands. Think of how he smiled!"

The King raised the flap of the tent with his own hand so as not to wake up the servant and he let the stranger out. The young man crossed the plain again steeped in thought, and as he went, he saw a large city blazing in flames on the horizon in the evening light.

He climbed over dead people and the decaying carcasses of horses until it grew dark and he reached the edge of the forest. Suddenly the great bird swooped down from the clouds and took the young man on its wings, and they flew through the night silently and softly like an owl.

When the young man awoke from a restless sleep, he lay in the small temple in the mountains, and his horse stood before the temple in the wet grass, greeting the day with a neigh.

The messenger recalled nothing of the great bird and his flight to a foreign planet. He recalled nothing of the King and the battlefield. All that remained was a shadow in his soul; a tiny, obscure pain as if from a sharp thorn.

It hurt, just as sympathy hurts when nothing can be done, just as a little unfulfilled wish can torment us in dreams until we finally encounter the person we have secretly loved and with whom we want to share our joy; the person whose smile we wish to see.

The messenger mounted his horse and rode the entire day until he came to the capital, where he was admitted to the King. He proved to be the right messenger for the King received him with a greeting of grace by touching his forehead and remarking, "Your request was fulfilled before I even heard it."

Soon, the messenger received a charter from the King that placed all the flowers of the whole country at his command. Companions and messengers went with him to the villages to pick them up.

Joined by wagons and horses, they took a few days to go around the mountain on the flat country road that led back to his province and community.

The young man led the wagons and carts, horses and donkeys, all loaded with the most beautiful flowers from gardens and greenhouses that were plentiful in the north.

There were enough flowers to place burial bouquets on the bodies of the dead and to adorn their graves lavishly, as well as enough to plant a memorial flower, a bush, and a young tree for each dead person.

The pain caused by the death of his friend and his favorite horse turned into silent, serene memories after he adorned and buried them and planted two flowers, two bushes, and two fruit trees over their graves.

Now that he had done what he had desired and fulfilled his obligations, the memory of that journey through the night began to stir in his soul. He asked his friends and relatives to permit him to spend a day all alone. He sat under the Tree of Contemplation one whole day and night. There he unfolded, clean and unwrinkled in his memory, the images of all that he had seen on the foreign planet.

One day later, he went to the Chief elder, requested a private talk, and told him all that had happened. The Chief elder sat and pondered everything as he listened. Then he asked, "Did you see all this with your eyes or was it a dream?"

"I don't know," said the young man. "I believe it may have been a dream. However, with your permission, may I say that it seems to me there is hardly a difference whether I actually experienced everything in reality.

A shadow of sadness has remained within me, and a cool wind from that other planet continues to blow upon me, right into the midst of the happiness of my life. That is why I am asking you, honorable Chief, what to do about this."

"Return to the mountains tomorrow," the Chief elder said, "and go up to the place where you found the temple. The symbol of that god seems odd to me, for I've never heard of it before. It may well be that he is a god from another star.

Or perhaps the temple and its god are so old that they belong to an epoch of our earliest ancestors, to those days when there are supposed to have been weapons, fear, and dread of death among us. Go to that temple, my dear boy, and bring flowers, honey, and song."

The young man thanked the Chief elder and followed his advice. He took a bowl of honey, such as was customarily presented to honored guests at the first festival of the bees in early summer, and carried his lute with him.

In the mountains he found the place where he had once picked the bluebell, and he found the steep rocky path in the forest that led up the mountain, where he had recently gone on foot leading his horse.

However, he could not find the place of the temple or the temple itself, the black sacrificial stone, the wooden pillars, the roof, or the great bird on the roof.

He could not find them on that day, nor on the next, and nobody he asked knew anything about the kind of temple that he described.

He returned to his home, and when he walked by the Shrine of Lovely Memories, he went inside. He offered the honey, played the lute and sang, and told the god of lovely memories all about his dream, the temple and the bird, the poor farmer, and the dead bodies on the battlefield. Most of all, he told about the King in his war tent.

Then he returned to his home with a light heart, Hanged the symbol of the unity of the world in his bedroom, and recuperated from the events of the past few days in deep sleep.

The next morning he helped his neighbors remove the last traces of the earthquake from the gardens and fields. They sang as they worked.

Faldum

Faldum was rich and its people were charming and neat. The country was filled with milk, honey, nuts, fruits, apples and meat, and most of its people were honest diligent law abiding citizens.

Like everywhere else, people felt satisfied and content as long as they prospered along with everybody else, but not much less. Most countries are much the same, as long as nothing out of the ordinary happens to them.

Faldum lay on a high plateau accessible through a long and upwardly winding road that travels through forests, green meadows and sometimes cornfields. As you get closer you would see farms, grazing cattle and small houses with gardens along the way.

Faldum's landscape consisted mainly of gentle hills, pretty little valleys, meadows, woods, farmlands and vegetable gardens. The sea was far below and too far to see.

Once a year, the people of Faldum used to organize a big fair in the capital. On that particular morning, the pretty road to Faldum saw livelier traffic both on foot and on horseback than at any other time of the year because this was the day of the great annual fair in the capital.

People of Faldum started thinking about the fair weeks before the great day. Craftsmen, apprentices, farmers, students, housewives, even servants and maids, dreamed of going there. But of course not everyone could go, some had to stay home, or on the farm, to look after the sick, the old, the little children, the cattle or the sheep.

Those who chose to stay to take care of the house and property felt as if they were losing almost a year of their life and bitterly resented the beautiful sun that shone warm and radiant, since early morning, in the late summer blue sky.

Everyone wore their Sunday clothes. Married women and girls hurried along with little baskets on their arms, the young men with clean-shaven cheeks had flowers in their buttonholes, and the schoolgirls' carefully braided their hair which shone wet and lustrous in the sunshine.

Those driving carriages had a flower or a red ribbon tied around the handles of their whips and, those who could afford it, decorated the harness of their horses with strings of brightly polished brass discs that reached to the horses' knees.

Rack wagons came by with green roofs of beech branches arching over them while people sat with baskets, or children in their laps singing loudly, in chorus, underneath.

Every now and then, a particularly cheerful wagon appeared with banners and red, blue, and white paper flowers among the green beech leaves. Lively village music swelled and echoed from the wagon with glinted and sparkled golden horns and trumpets darting between the beech branches.

Little children, who were dragged along since sunrise, began to cry and were comforted by their perspiring mothers, many were given lifts by friendly drivers.

An old woman was pushing twins in a baby carriage, both falling asleep with round and rosy cheeks. On the pillow between the two sleeping children lay two beautifully dressed and combed dolls.

Those staying home and did not go to the fair were few in number, but still, everyone living along the road had an entertaining morning with the continuous procession of sights and sounds.

A ten-year-old boy sat weeping on garden chair because he had to remain with his grandmother, but when he saw a couple of village boys trotting past he decided that he wept long enough and ran down to the road and joined them.

Not far from where the boy lived, an elderly bachelor didn't want to hear a thing about the fair because he resented spending his money. He had already planned to trim the high thorn hedge around his garden in peace and quiet, while everybody else was away celebrating that day.

As the morning dew began to evaporate, he went cheerily to work with his long hedge shears. All those who passed by looked at him in astonishment as he was trimming his hedge and made jokes about his ill-timed diligence.

Young girls giggled when he threatened them furiously with his long shears and everyone waved their hats and laughed at him. He stopped his hedge trimming exercise and went angrily back inside his house. Sitting there, behind closed shutters, he kept on peering out enviously through the cracks at the passers by.

His anger subsided as the last few passers by bustled and hurried along, as though their lives depended on getting there on time. He pulled on his boots, put some change in his pocket, picked up his walking stick and was ready to follow the others. He locked the house and the garden gate and ran so fast that he reached the city ahead of many of those who walked and even overtook some heavy wagons.

Eventually, the dust began to gently settle over the

road and the sound of hoofs and the band music faded away in the distance. The road lay empty and hot and a few sparrows came out of the fields and surveyed what was left over from the commotion. From time to time, a shout or the notes of a horn could be faintly heard from the far distance.

A man strolled out of the forest, his broad-brimmed hat pulled low over his eyes. He was tall and had the firm quiet stride of a hiker who has traveled great distances on foot. He wandered unhurriedly alone along the empty road.

The man was dressed inconspicuously in gray. Out of the shadow of his hat his eyes peered attentive and calm, the eyes of one who desires nothing more from the world but observes everything scrupulously and overlooks nothing.

He took note of the many confused wagon tracks running along the road and the hoof marks of a horse that had thrown the shoe from its left back foot. Through the dusty haze in the distance he saw the roofs of the city of Faldum, small and shimmering.

He saw a tiny old woman, full of anxiety and fear, rushing around a garden on the top of a hill and calling to someone who did not answer. On the edge of the road, the sun flashed from a piece of metal, he bent and picked up a bright round brass disc that had come from a horse's collar and put it in his pocket.

Then he saw an old thorn hedge on the side of the road with a few paces freshly trimmed. Part of the work seemed neat and precise as if executed with pleasure, but with each half stride it grew less even and soon a cut had gone too deep, neglected twigs were sticking up bristly and thorny.

Farther on, the stranger found a child's doll lying in the road with its head crushed by a wagon wheel, beside it, he saw a piece of rye bread still gleaming with melted butter. Then he found a leather purse with a silver coin inside. He rested the doll against a curb, crumbled the slice of bread and fed it to the sparrows and put the coin purse in his pocket.

The abandoned road was rather quiet and the turf on either side lay gray and covered with dust. In the nearby farmyard the chickens ran around with no one to mind, cackling and stuttering dreamily in the warm sun.

An old woman was stooping over a bluish cabbage patch pulling weeds out of the dry soil. The wanderer called to her to ask how far it was to the city, but she seemed deaf. When he called louder she only looked at him helplessly and shook her gray head.

From time to time, music reached him from the city as he walked on, swelling and then dying away, then more often and for longer periods, then it sounded uninterruptedly like a distant waterfall. Then he heard a confusion of voices, as though a congress of mankind was happily assembled up there.

A stream now ran beside the road, broad and quiet, with ducks swimming on it and brownish-green weed under the blue surface. Then the road began a steeper climb and the stream curved to one side; a stone bridge led across it.

A thin man who looked like a tailor was sitting asleep with drooping head on the low wall of the bridge; his hat had fallen off into the dust and beside him sat a droll little dog keeping watch.

The wanderer was about to wake up the sleeper, concerned that he might fall off the wall of the bridge during his sleep, but as he looked down he saw that the height was moderate and the water shallow. He let the tailor go on sleeping undisturbed.

After the short steep rise in the road the wanderer came to the gate of the city of Faldum. The gate stood wide open with no one in sight. He strode through the gate, his steps resounding suddenly and loudly on the paved street. In front of the houses on both sides of the street, there were rows of empty unharnessed wagons.

Only the upper windows of the houses reflected the golden day but the little street lay empty in the shadow. There was no one in sight, but noise and confused shouting came through from other streets.

The wanderer sat down on the pole of a rack wagon for a short rest, placed the brass harness decoration he had found on the road on the driver's seat, then he got up and continued further down the street.

As he walked around the block he got engulfed in the noise and confusion of the fair. Dealers loudly hawking their wares in a hundred booths, butchers fishing long necklaces of fresh wet sausages out of huge boiling kettles and children blowing on silvery trumpets.

On a high platform, peering encouragingly through thick horn-rimmed glasses, stood a quack pointing to a chart on which there were inscribed all sorts of human diseases and ailments.

A man with long black hair leading a camel by a rope walked past as the camel twisted its divided lips back and forth as it chewed and looked arrogantly down its long neck on the bustling crowd below.

The wanderer allowed himself to be pushed and shoved along by the people while looking attentively at all this, absorbing the scene, glancing now into the stand of a dealer of colored prints, then reading sayings and mottoes on sugared gingerbread. He lingered nowhere and seemed as if he probably hasn't found what he was looking for yet.

As he proceeded slowly he arrived at the big central square. On one corner, a bird dealer had a shop. He listened to the voices that came from the many little cages for a while, then he answered them whistling softly to the linnet, the quail, the canary, the warbler.

Suddenly he saw a bright flash of light nearby, as brilliant and blinding as though all the sunshine had been concentrated at this one point. As he approached, it turned out to be a big mirror hanging in an exhibitor's booth.

There were dozens of other mirrors beside it; big, small, rectangular, round and oval. There were mirrors hanging on walls, mirrors on stands, hand mirrors and little narrow pocket mirrors that you carry with you so you wouldn't forget how you looked like. The dealer stood in front of his booth manipulating a sparkling hand mirror and reflecting the sun in dancing patterns around his booth and he kept on shouting tirelessly:

"Mirrors, ladies and gentlemen. This is the place to buy mirrors! The best mirrors, the cheapest mirrors in Faldum! Mirrors, ladies, magnificent mirrors! Just take a look at them, all genuine, all of the best crystal!"

Among the people inspecting the mirrors there were three young fresh and healthy peasant girls dressed in white stockings and thick-soled shoes. The three had blonde and eager young eyes. The wanderer stopped, as if he had found what he was looking for, and took up a position beside the mirror booth close to the peasant girls.

Each of the girls held a small cheap mirror in her hand. They seemed hesitant about making a purchase but enjoying a pleasurable torment of choice. Each would gaze dreamily into the clear depths of the mirror, surveying her image, her mouth and eyes, the little ornament at her throat, the sprinkling of freckles across the bridge of her nose, the smooth hair and the rosy ear.

As they became silent and solemn; the wanderer who was standing just behind them saw their large-eyed, serious faces peering out of the three mirrors.

"Oh, how I wish I had hair that was all red-gold and long enough to reach to my knees!" he heard the first one say.

Hearing her friend's wish, the second girl sighed softly and looked more intently into her mirror. Then, blushing, she timidly revealed what her heart dreamed: "If I had a wish, I would like to have the prettiest hands, all white and delicate, with long narrow fingers and rosy fingernails."

She glanced down at the hand that was holding the oval mirror. Her hands were not ugly but they were rather short and broad and had become roughened and coarse from manual work.

The third, the smallest and merriest of the three, laughed gaily and said "That's not a bad wish. But you know hands aren't so important. What I'd like most is to be, from today on, the best and nimblest dancer in the whole country of Faldum."

Then the girl gave a sudden start and turned around, for out of the mirror, behind her own face, peered a stranger's face with gleaming black eyes. It was the face of the wanderer. None of the three girls had seen him standing behind them until that moment.

They stared at him with amazement as he nodded and said "Young ladies, you have made three nice wishes, are you really serious about them?"

The small girl had put down the mirror and hidden her hands behind her back. She wanted to pay the man back for startling her and was trying to think of a sharp rejoinder. But when she looked into his face, there was such power in his eyes that she got confused.

"Is it any business of yours what I wish?" was all she could say, blushing.

The girl who wished for beautiful hands was impressed by the tall man's dignified and fatherly air and she said: "Yes, indeed, I am serious about it. Could one wish for anything finer?"

The mirror dealer approached and other people started listening. The wanderer pushed back the brim of his hat so that his smooth high forehead and imperious eyes were strikingly visible. Then he nodded and smiled at the three girls and said "Look, look, now you have everything you've wished for!"

The girls stared at one another, then each looked quickly into a mirror, and they all grew pale with astonishment and joy. The first one had thick gold locks reaching to her knees. The second held her mirror in the whitest, slimmest princess hands, and the third was suddenly standing in red leather dancing shoes on ankles as slim as those of a deer.

They could not grasp what happened, but the one with the beautiful hands burst into blissful tears, leaned on the shoulder next to her, and wept happily into her friend's long hair. People began shouting news of the miracle from the neighborhood of the booth. A young journeyman who had seen the whole thing stood there staring at the stranger with wide open eyes as though he had turned to stone.

"Wouldn't you like to wish something for yourself?" the wanderer asked the young journeyman. The apprentice gave a start, became totally confused, and let his eyes rove about helplessly, trying to find something he could wish for. Then he saw a large string of thick red sausages hanging in front of a butcher's booth and he stammered pointing at it: "A string of sausages like these. That's what I'd like to have!"

And behold, there the string of sausages hung around his neck, and all who saw it began to laugh and shout.

Everyone tried to press closer, everyone wanted to make a wish, and they were all allowed.

The next to have a turn was a blacksmith who wished for a new outfit from top to toe. The man hardly spoke when he found himself dressed in a brand new suit as fine as the mayor's.

Then came a country woman who took her courage in both hands and asked straight out for five silver coins. Instantly, the coins were jingling in her purse.

Now people saw that in all truth miracles were happening and the news started spreading from the marketplace across the city and a huge group quickly formed around the booth of the mirror dealer.

Few were still laughing and joking, made skeptical remarks and wouldn't believe a word of it. But many succumbed to the wish fever and came rushing with glowing eyes and with faces hot and contorted with greed and worry, each fearing that the source might dry up before he had a chance to participate.

Boys wished for cookies, crossbows, dogs, bags full of nuts, books, and games of bowls. Girls went away happy with new clothes, ribbons, gloves, and parasols.

A little ten-year-old boy who had run away from his grandmother and was quite beside himself with the sheer splendor and glamor of the fair wished in a clear voice for a black horse. Immediately, black colt appeared and started rubbing its head affectionately on the boy's shoulder.

An elderly bachelor quivering with excitement and hardly able to speak a word forced his way through the miracle-intoxicated crowd with a walking stick in his hand. "I wi-wish,' he stammered, 'I wi-wish for myself two hundred ---"

The wanderer looked at him closely, took a leather coin purse from his pocket, held it in front of the excited man's eyes and said: "Wait a minute! Was it you who lost this purse with a silver coin in?"

"Yes, I certainly did. That's mine." replied the bachelor.

"Do you want it back?"

"Yes, yes, I want it back, give it back to me!"

Once the bachelor got his purse back he realized that he'd just used up his wish. He became furious and went at the wanderer trying to hit him with his walking-stick but he missed and knocked down one of the mirrors instead. As the glass fragments scattered rattling on the floor the mirror dealer appeared and demanded compensation and the old bachelor had to pay.

Then a short beer-bellied man came forward and made a wish of a new roof for his house. Immediately brand-new tiles and white washed chimneys appeared shining in his street.

Everyone became feverish and their wishes were pitched higher. Soon there was a man who felt no shame in making the modest wish for a new four-story house on the market-place. In a quarter of an hour he was leaning over his own windowsill and watching the fair from that vantage point.

It was now really no longer a fair, instead all the life of the city, like a river from a spring, flowed only from that spot beside the mirror booth where one could get a wish from the wanderer. Cries of wonder, envy, or derision greeted each wish. When a hungry little boy wished for nothing but a hat full of plums, his hat was filled again with silver coins by someone who made a less modest wish.

Great rejoicing and applause broke out when the fat wife of a shopkeeper made use of her wish to cure herself of a large goiter. Then came an example of what anger and jealousy can do. The woman's husband, who lived in conflict with her and had just had a fight with her, made use of his own wish, which might have made him rich, to restore the vanished goiter to its old place.

But the precedent had been set, and crowds of the sick and infirm were fetched and people fell into new frenzies as the lame began to dance and the blind ecstatically greeted the light with reawakened eyes.

Youngsters ran about everywhere announcing the miraculous happenings. The story was told of a loyal old cook hearing the news through the open kitchen window while standing at the oven roasting a goose for her employer and how she couldn't resist running off to the marketplace in order to wish herself a rich and happy life.

But the farther along she pressed in the crowd the more tormented her conscience became. When it was her turn to make wish, she gave up her original plan and only requested that the goose might not burn up before she got back home.

The frenzy would not end. Nursing mothers came rushing out of their houses with babies in their arms and invalids stormed the streets in their nightgowns. In a state of great confusion and despair, a tiny old lady made her way in from the country and when she heard about the wishing she begged in tears that she might find her lost grandchild safe and sound. Without an instant's delay there came the boy riding on a little black horse and fell laughing into her arms.

Finally the whole city was transformed and overcome by intoxication. Pairs of lovers, their wishes fulfilled, wandered happily arm in arm. Families rode in wagons, still wearing the old mended clothes they had put on that morning.

Many, already regretting their unwise wishes, either sadly disappeared or drank themselves into forgetfulness at the old fountain in the marketplace which was springing fine white wine instead of water, as per one prankster's wish.

In the whole city of Faldum there were only two people who knew nothing about the miracle and had made no wishes for themselves. They were two young men who lived behind closed windows high up in an attic room of an old house on the edge of town.

One of them stood in the middle of the room with a violin under his chin and played with utter surrender of body and soul and the other sat in a corner with his head in his hands totally absorbed in listening.

Through the little windowpanes, the beams of the late afternoon sun obliquely lit a bunch of flowers standing on the table and played over the torn wallpaper. The room was completely suffused with warm light and the glowing tones of the violin, like a little secret treasure chamber filled with the glitter of gems.

The violinist's eyes were closed and he swayed back and forth as he played. The listener stared at the floor, lost in the music, as motionless as though there were no life in him. Then footsteps sounded in the street and the house gate was thrown open and someone pounded heavily up the stairs all the way to the attic room. It was the owner of the house, who tore the door open and came shouting and laughing into the room.

The music abruptly ceased; the silent listener leaped up startled and distressed, the violinist too was angry at being disturbed. But the landlord paid no attention, he swung his arms about like a drunkard and shouted:

"Fools, there you sit fiddling and outside the whole world is being changed. Wake up and run so you won't be too late. There's a man in the marketplace who makes a wish come true for everyone. So you needn't live under the roof any more and continue to owe me the miserable bit of rent. Up and away before it's too late! I too have become a rich man today."

The violinist heard this with astonishment, but since the man would not leave him in peace, he set his violin aside and put his hat on his head. His friend followed silently.

They were barely out of the house when they saw the most remarkable changes in the city. They walked bemused, as though in a dream, past houses that only yesterday had been gray and mean but now stood tall and elegant as palaces.

People they had known as beggars drove by in four-horse carriages or looked in proud affluence out of the windows of beautiful homes. An emaciated fellow, who looked like a tailor and was followed by a tiny dog, was sweating as he wearily dragged behind him a great heavy sack, from which gold pieces trickled through a small hole on to the pavement.

As though drawn by some magnet, the two youths arrived in the marketplace and in front of the booth with the mirrors where the wanderer stood. "You're in no hurry with your wishes. I was just about to leave. Well, tell me what you want and don't feel any hesitation.", he said.

The violinist shook his head and said: "Oh, if they'd only left me alone! I don't want anything."

"You don't? Think again!" cried the wanderer. "You may wish for anything at all, anything you can think of."

The violinist closed his eyes for a moment and reflected. Then he said softly: "I would like a violin on which I could play so marvelously that the whole world with its uproar could no longer come near me."

And behold, he was already holding a priceless violin and a bow in his hands, and he tucked the violin under his chin and began to play: it sang sweet and strong songs of Paradise.

Whoever heard it stopped and listened and his eyes grew solemn. But the violinist, playing more and more intensely and beautifully, was swept away from those who became invisible and disappeared in the air. Still from a great distance his music came drifting back with a soft radiance like the glow of sunset.

"And you? What do you wish for yourself?" the wanderer asked the other young man. "Now you have taken the violinist away from me!" the youth said. "I want nothing from life but to listen and watch, and I would like to think only about what is immortal. And so I would like to be a mountain as big as the countryside of Faldum and so tall that my summit would tower above the clouds."

Then a quickening began beneath the earth and everything started to shudder. There was a sound of breaking glass, the mirrors fell one after another into splinters on the pavement, and the marketplace rose swaying like a cloth under which a cat has suddenly awakened and arched its back.

An immense terror seized the people, thousands fled screaming out of the city into the fields. But those who remained in the square saw behind the city a mighty mountain rising up into the evening clouds, and they saw the quiet stream transformed into a wild white torrent that rushed down foaming from high up on the mountain, with many falls and rapids, into the valley below.

The whole countryside of Faldum turned into a gigantic mountain with the city lying at its foot, and one could see the ocean from afar. No one was injured. An old man who saw the whole thing from beside the mirror booth said to his neighbor: "The world's gone mad. I'm glad I don't have much longer to live. I'm just sorry about the violinist, would have liked to hear him play once more."

"Yes, indeed," said the other. "But tell me, what happened to the strange man?"

They looked around but he was not there. When they gazed up at the new mountain they saw the wanderer walking away, his cape waving in the wind; he stood for an instant, gigantic against the evening sky, then he vanished behind a cliff.

Everything perishes, and all new things grow old. The annual fair became a thing of the past, and many a man who had wished himself rich on that occasion had long since grown poor again.

The girl with the long red-gold hair got married and had children, who visited the fair themselves every summer.

The girl with the nimble dancing feet married a master workman, she grew old but she still could dance better than many young people. Her husband, who wished himself a great deal of money, managed to spend it all during their lifetime.

The girl with the beautiful hands neither got rich nor got married, but she managed to keep her hands delicate and stopped doing farm work. She tended children in the village whenever she was needed and told them fairy tales and stories; it was from her that all the children learned about the miraculous fair and how the poor became rich and how the countryside of Faldum became a mountain.

When she told these stories she used to look smilingly at her slender princess hands. She looked so lively and charming that one could believe there had been no luckier or more splendid prize given out at the mirror booth than hers.

Everyone who was young at that time became now old, and whoever was old then was now dead. Only the mountain was unaltered and ageless, and when the snow sparkled through the clouds on his summit, he seemed to smile and was happy that he was no longer a man and did not have to think in terms of human time.

He stood high above the city with shining cliffs, his huge shadow spread every day across the land and his streams and rivers brought down advance notice of the waxing and waning of the seasons.

The mountain became the protector and father of all. Forests grew on him along with meadows with waving grass and flowers. Springs gushed forth from his with snow and stones, and on the stones grew bright moss and beside the streams lovely flowers grew.

There were caverns within the mountain where, with delicious music, water dripped in silver threads from stone to stone, and there were secret chambers where, with millennial patience, crystals grew.

No man had ever stood on the mountain's top, but many claimed to know that up there at his summit was a small round lake in which nothing had ever been mirrored except the sun, the moon, the clouds, and the stars. Neither man nor animal had ever looked into this pool which the mountain held up to the heavens. Even eagles could not fly so high.

The people of Faldum lived happily in their city and in the many valleys. They baptized their children, they conducted trade and commerce, and they carried one another to the grave. Their knowledge and their dreams about the mountain was handed on from forefathers to grandchildren and continued as a living tradition. Shepherds and chamois hunters, naturalists and botanists, cow herders and travelers increased the treasure, and the makers of songs and tellers of tales spread it abroad.

They learned of endless dark caves, of sunless waterfalls in hidden chasms, of towering glaciers, they learned the paths of the avalanches and the tricks of the weather, and everything the land received by way of warmth and frost, water and growth, weather and wind, all came from the mountain.

No one any longer knew about the earlier times. To be sure, there was the beautiful saga of the miraculous annual fair, at which each soul in Faldum was allowed to make a wish, but no one would now believe that the mountain was formed on that day.

They knew for certain that the mountain stood in its place from the beginning of time and would remain there for all eternity. The mountain was home, the mountain was Faldum.

The people loved to hear the stories about the three girls and about the violin player, and every once in awhile, a youth would lock his door and lose himself in his violin playing as he dreamed of vanishing in his most beautiful song like that violin player who was swept away into heaven.

The mountain lived on, silent and immense. Each day he saw the sun rise red and distant out of the ocean and saw it pursue its circular course past his summit from east to west, and each night he watched the stars follow the same silent track.

Each winter covered him with heavy snow and ice, and each spring avalanches thundered on their way down, as bright-eyed summer flowers laughed in the sun, at the edges of their melting snow, and the lakes shone blue and warm in the sun-light.

The small round lake high above on the summit would remain under heavy ice all year but for the brief period of high summer when for a few days it would open its bright blue eye to the sun and, for a few nights, reflect the stars.

In the mountain's dark caverns, where music resounded of water drops unceasing fall on the stones, thousand-year-old crystals grew steadfastly towards perfection in secret shafts.

A little higher than the city, a valley lay at the foothills of the mountain and a broad stream with a smooth surface flowed between alders and willows. Young people in love went there and learned the marvel of the seasons from the mountain and the trees. In another valley men trained with horses and weapons, and on a high steep promontory a mighty fire burned each year during the night of the summer solstice.

Ages slipped by and the mountain safeguarded the lovers' valley and the field of arms. He gave a home to cowherds and woodsmen, hunters and lumbermen. It provided stone for building and iron for smelting.

Indifferent and permissive, he watched the first summer fire blaze on the promontory and saw it return a hundred times and many hundred times again. He saw the city down below reach out with little stumpy arms and grow beyond his ancient walls.

He saw the hunters discard their crossbows and take up firearms. The centuries ran past him like the seasons of the year, and the years like hours. It caused him no concern that, in the long course of years, a time came when the red solstice fire did not blaze on the smooth rock and then remained forgotten.

He was not worried when, in the march of the ages, the field of arms was deserted and was taken over by thorn flowers. And he did nothing to interfere when, in the long course of the centuries, a landslide altered his form and half the city of Faldum was reduced to rubble under the thundering rocks.

He barely glanced down and did not even notice that the city lay there in ruins and no one rebuilt it. All this disturbed him not at all. But something else did begin to worry him. The ages had slipped by and, behold, the mountain had grown old.

When he saw the sun rise and move across the sky and depart, it was not the way it had once been, and when he saw the stars reflected in the pale glaciers he no longer felt himself their equal.

Neither the sun nor the stars were any longer important to him. What was important now was what was happening to himself and within himself. For he could feel deep beneath his cliffs and caverns an alien hand at work, hard primitive rock grew friable and weathered into flaky slates as streams and waterfalls ate their way deeper.

The glaciers disappeared, the lakes broadened and the forests turned into fields full of stones. The meadows turned into black non-arable land with silt and rocks extending far out into the country in pointed tongues. The landscape below became strangely altered, oddly stony, blasted and silent. The mountain withdrew more and more into himself.

He was clearly no longer the equal of the sun and the stars, his equals were wind and snow, water and ice. Whatever seemed eternal and yet slowly worn away and perished, that was his equal. He began to guide his streams more affectionately down into the valley, he rolled his avalanches with greater caution, he offered his flowery meadows more solicitously to the sun.

In his advanced age he remembered men again, not that he thought of them as equals, but he began to search for them. He felt abandoned and thought about the past, but the city was no longer there and there were no more songs in the valley of love nor huts on the mountain peaks. There were no more men. All was gone. All dried out, all grew still and a shadow lay in the air.

The mountain shuddered when he realized what dissolution meant. As he shuddered, his summit bent to one side and pitched down. Rocky fragments rolled down across the valley of love, long since filled up with stones, and down into the sea.

Times had changed. Why was it that just now he remembered men and thought about them continually? It was beautiful once when the fire on the high land burned and the young people wandered in pairs through the valley of love? And oh, how sweet and warm their songs sounded!

The ancient mountain was wholly sunk in memories, he hardly noticed the centuries flowing by, how here and there in his caverns there was subsidence accompanied by collisions and a soft thundering.

When he thought about men he was pained by a dull echo from past ages of the world, a vague inclination and love, a dim intermittent dream as though once he too had been a man or like men, had sung and heard others sing, as though the idea of mortality had once in his earliest days transfixed his heart.

The ages flowed by. Collapsing, surrounded by a barren wasteland of rubble, the dying mountain gave himself up to his dreams. Thought about the past, searching for some remaining resonance, slender silver threads that united him with a bygone world. He burrowed in the night of mouldering memories, groping ceaselessly for torn threads, repeatedly bending far out over the abyss of things past.

He thought of the distant past, hadn't there been a glow of friendship, of love, for him too? Hadn't he too, the lonely one, the great one, once been an equal among equals? Hadn't there been once, at the beginning of the world, a mother who sang to him?

He brooded and brooded, and his eyes, the blue lakes, grew cloudy and dull and turned into moor and swamp, and over the strips of grass and little patches of flowers swept the rolling boulders.

He continued to brood, and from an unimaginable distance he heard a chime ringing, felt the notes of music around him, a song, a human song, and he trembled with the painful joy of recognition. He heard the notes and he saw a man, a youth, wholly enveloped in music, poised in mid-air in the sunny sky, and a hundred buried memories were aroused and began to quiver and stir.

He saw a human face with dark eyes, and the eyes asked commandingly: "Don't you want to make a wish?"

And he made a wish, a silent wish, and as he did, he was freed from the torment of having to think about all those lost and distant things and everything that caused him pain fell from him.

The mountain collapsed and with it the country, and where Faldum had been, the endless sea tossed and roared, and over it in steady alternation moved the sun and the stars.

Iris

When Anselm was still a young boy, he used to run and play in his mother's garden. The sword lily was his favorite flower. He used to gaze at it for ages, touch its spikes with his exploring fingers, press his cheek against its tall bright green leaves and inhale the scent of its marvelous blooms.

Inside its cup, there were long rows of yellow fingers rising from its pale blue flowering floor and between them ran a bright path far downward into its chalice and through the remote blue mystery of its blossom.

Anselm had a great love for this flower and peering into it was his favorite pastime. Sometimes he saw the delicate upright yellow members as a golden fence in a king's garden and sometimes as a double row of beautiful dream trees untouched by any breeze.

Between them, bright and interlaced with living veins as delicate as glass, ran the mysterious path to its interior.

There at the back, the cavern yawned hugely and the path between the golden trees lost itself in an infinitely deep unimaginable abyss where the violet vault arched royally above and cast thin magic shadows on the silent expectant marvel.

Anselm knew that this was the flower's mouth, that behind the luxuriant yellow finery in the blue abyss lived the flower's heart and thoughts, and that along this lovely shining path with its glassy veins her breath and dreams flowed to and fro.

Around the tall flower stood smaller ones that were not yet open. They rose on firm stems in little cups of brownish-yellow skin, out of which the new blossoms forced their way upward silently and vigorously.

Even these young tight-rolled petals showed a network of veins and a hundred secret signs. Erect, neatly rolled and wrapped tight in bright-green and lilac with new deep violet at the very top, they peered out in delicate points.

When he came out of the house every morning fresh from sleep and dreams and strange worlds, there stood the garden waiting for him, never lost yet always new.

Where yesterday he saw the tightly rolled hard blue point of a blossom staring out of its green sheath, now he saw a young petal with a tongue and a lip hung thin and blue as air tentatively searching for the curving form of which it had long dreamed.

The bright veined path and the far-off fragrant abyss of the soul still engaged in a noiseless struggle with its sheath at the very bottom where delicate yellow growth was already in preparation.

As early as midday, perhaps by evening, it would open, the blue silky tent would unfold over the golden forest and her first dreams, thoughts and songs would be breathed silently out of the magical abyss.

There came a day when the grass was full of blue bell-flowers. There came a day when suddenly there were new sounds and a new fragrance in the garden and the first tea rose hung soft and golden red over the sun-drenched leaves.

There came a day when there were no more sword lilies. They were gone! There were no more gold-fenced paths leading gently down into fragrant mysteries and the cool pointed leaves stood stark and unfriendly.

There came a day when red berries were ripening in the bushes and new joyous reddish-brown butterflies with mother-of-pearl backs and whirring glassy wings flew unconfined above the star flowers.

Anselm talked to the butterflies and the pebbles and made friends with the beetles and lizards. Birds told him bird stories, ferns secretly revealed to him under the roof of their giant leaves their stores of brown seeds.

For him fragments of green and crystal glass, catching the sun's rays, turned into palaces, gardens, and sparkling treasure chambers.

With the lilies gone, the nasturtiums bloomed; when the tea roses wilted, then brambles grew brown. Everything changed places, was always there and always gone, disappeared and came again in its season.

Even during those marvelous frightening days when the wind whistled chilly through the pine forest and the wilted foliage rattled scorched and dead in the garden, a new experience arose bringing still another story, another song.

When all subsided, snow fell outside the windows and palm forests grew on the panes. Angels with silver bells flew through the evening and hall and attic smelled sweetly of dried fruit.

Friendship and confidence never failed in that good world. And when snow-drops unexpectedly shone beside the black ivy leaves, then it was as though they had been there all the time.

Until one day, never expected and yet always exactly the way it had to be and always equally welcome, the first pointed bluish bud peeped out again from the stem of the sword lily.

To Anselm everything was beautiful, everything was delightful, friendly, and familiar, but his highest moment of magic and of grace came each year with the first sword lily.

Other flowers too had mouths, others diffused fragrance and thoughts, others too enticed bees and beetles into their small sweet chambers. But the blue lily had become dearer and more important to him than any other flower.

The sword lily accompanied Anselm through all the years of his innocence and, with each new summer it came back new, more moving and richer in mystery.

For him, she was the symbol and example of everything worth contemplating and marveling at. At some moment in his earliest childhood he had read in her chalice for the first time the book of marvels, her fragrance and changing multifarious blue had been summons and key to the universe.

Each phenomenon on earth is an allegory and each allegory is an open gate through which, if ready, the soul can pass into the interior of the world where you and I and day and night are all one.

In the course of life, every human being comes upon that open gate where everyone gets surprised by the thought that everything visible is an allegory and that behind the allegory live spirit and eternal life.

Few, to be sure, pass through the gate and give up the beautiful illusion for the perceived reality of what lies within.

To Anselm, the chalice of his flower seemed to be the open unvoiced question towards which his soul was striving in anticipation of an answer.

When he gazed into her chalice in absorption, and allowed his thoughts to follow that bright dreamlike path between the marvelous yellow shrubbery towards the twilight interior, his soul looked through the gate where appearance becomes a paradox and seeing a surmise.

Sometimes at night he dreamed of this flowery chalice, saw it opening gigantically in front of him like the gate of a heavenly palace, and through it, he would ride on horseback or would fly on swans.

With him flew and rode and glided gently the whole world drawn by magic into the lovely abyss, inward and downward, where every expectation had to find fulfillment and every intimation came true.

Anselm would often sit with closed eyes and contemplate himself. He would marvel at his own body and at the strange sensations, impulses, and intimations in his mouth and throat, as he swallowed, as he sang and as he breathed.

He would grope for the path and the gate by which soul can go to soul. With amazement, he would observe the colored figures, full of meaning, which would appear to him out of the purple darkness when he closed his eyes, spots and half circles of blue and deep red with glassy-bright lines between.

Sometimes he would realize, with a happy start, the subtle hundredfold interconnections between eye and ear, smell and taste. He would feel, for beautiful fleeting instants, tones, noises, and letters of the alphabet related and very similar to red and blue or to hard and soft.

He would marvel, as he smelled some plant or peelings of green bark, at how strangely close smell and taste lie together and often cross over into one another and become one.

Then the lovely multiplicity of things drew him away again, in conversation and games with glass and stones, roots, bushes, animals, and all the friendly presences of his world.

All children feel this, although not all with the same intensity and delicacy. With many the feeling is gone, as though it had never existed, even before they've learned to read their first letters. Others retain the mystery of childhood for a long time, its vestige and echo stays with them into the days of white hair and weariness.

All children, as long as they remain within this mystery, are uninterruptedly occupied in their souls with the single important thing, with themsclves and their paradoxical-relationship to the outside world.

Seekers and wise men return to this preoccupation in their mature years. Most people, however, forget and abandon this inner world of the truly important, sometimes early and for good.

Most people would wander all their lives about the many-colored mazes of wishes, worries, and goals, that none of which had a place in their innermost being and that none of which would lead them back to their innermost being or to home.

During Anselm's childhood, summers and autumns softly came and went, again and again the snowdrops, wallflowers, violets, lilies, periwinkles, and roses bloomed and faded, beautiful and luxuriant as always.

He lived together with them; flower and bird, tree and spring listened to him, and he took his first written letters and the first woes of friendship in his old fashion way to the garden, to his mother, to the many colored stones that bordered the flower beds.

Then came a spring that did not sound and smell like all the earlier ones. The blackbird sang and it was not the old song, the blue iris bloomed and no dreams or fairy tales drifted out and in along the gold-fenced pathway of its chalice.

Strawberries laughed in hiding from among the green shadows, butterflies tumbled magnificently above the woodbine, but nothing was any longer the way it had always been; Anselm had other interests.

He did not know what the trouble was or why it hurted so, why something was always bothering him. He only saw that the world had changed, that the friendships of earlier times had fallen away and left him alone, and that he was frequently at odds with his mother.

A year passed, and then another, and Anselm was no longer a child. The colored stones around the flower-beds bored him, the flowers were silent, and he kept the beetles in a case, impaled on pins.

The old joys had dried up and withered, and his soul began a long hard detour. Boisterously the young man made his way into life, which seemed to him to have just begun. Blown away and forgotten was the world of allegory. New desires and new paths enticed him.

In his blue eyes and soft hair, the aura of childhood still lingered but he was irritated when reminded of it and had his hair cut short and adopted a bold and worldly air.

He stormed through the troubling secondary-school years, sometimes a good student and friend, sometimes alone and withdrawn, now buried in books until late at night, now wild and noisy at his youthful drinking bouts.

He left home and saw it only on brief occasions when he came to visit his mother. He changed a lot, grew tall and dressed handsomely. He would bring friends or books with him, always different ones, and when he walked through the old garden, it was small and silent under his distraught glance.

He no longer read stories in the many colored veins of the stones and the leaves, he no longer saw God and eternity dwelling in the blue secrecy of the iris blossom.

Then he went to college; came home with a red cap and then with a yellow one, with fuzz on his upper lip and then with a youthful beard. He brought with him foreign language books and one time a dog. In a letter case in his pocket he sometimes carried secret poems, the sayings of ancient wise men, or pictures of pretty girls and letters from them.

He came back from travels in distant lands and from sea voyages on great ships. He came back again and was a young teacher, wearing a black hat and dark gloves, and his old neighbors tipped their hats and called him professor although he was not yet one.

Once more he came home wearing black clothes and walked slim and solemn behind the slowly moving funeral car in which his old mother lay in a flower-covered coffin. After that he seldom returned.

In the city where he was now a teacher and had a high academic reputation, Anselm went about behaving exactly like other people of the world. He wore a fine hat and coat, he was serious or genial as the occasion demanded and he observed the world with alert but rather weary eyes. He was a gentleman and a scholar just as he wished to be.

Then things took a new turn for him, very much as they did at the end of his childhood. He suddenly felt as if many years had slipped past and left him standing strangely alone and unsatisfied with a way of life for which he had always longed.

It was no real happiness to be a professor, it was not really gratifying to be respectfully greeted by citizens and students, it was all stale and commonplace.

Happiness once more lay far in the future and the road there looked hot and dusty and tiresome.

Anselm often visited the house of a friend whose sister he found attractive. He was no longer inclined to run after pretty faces; in this too he had changed, and he felt that happiness for him must come in some special fashion and was not to be expected behind every window.

His friend's sister pleased him greatly and he often

thought that he loved her. But she was a strange girl; her every gesture, every word, bore her own stamp and coloring, and it was not always easy to keep pace with her in exactly the same rhythm.

During the evenings when he walked up and down in his lonely home, reflectively listening to his own footsteps echoing through the empty rooms, he struggled a great deal within himself about this woman.

She was older than he would have wished his wife to be. She was odd, and it would be difficult to live with her and pursue his academic ambitions, with which she had no sympathy at all.

She was not very robust or healthy and could not easily endure company or parties. By preference she lived in lonely quiet amid flowers, music, and books, letting the world go its way or come to her if it must. Sometimes her sensitivity was so acute that when something alien wounded her she would burst into tears.

Then again she would glow with some silent and secret happiness, and anyone who saw her would think how difficult it would be to give anything to this strange beautiful woman that would mean anything to her.

Sometimes Anselm believed she loved him, sometimes it seemed to him that she loved no one but was simply gentle and friendly with everyone and wanted nothing but to be left in peace.

Anselm demanded something quite different from life, and if he were to marry, then there must be life and excitement and hospitality in his home.

"Iris," he said to her, "dear Iris, if only the world was differently arranged! If nothing at all existed but your beautiful gentle world of flowers, thoughts, and music, then I too would wish for nothing at all but to spend my whole life with you, to hear your stories and to share in your thoughts. Your very name does me good. Iris is a wonderful name, and I have no idea what it reminds me of."

"But you do know," she said, "that the blue and yellow sword lilies are called that."

"Yes," he replied with an uneasy feeling. "I know it very well and that in itself is beautiful. But always when I pronounce your name it seems to remind me of something else, I don't know what, as though it were connected with some very deep, distant, important memories, and yet I don't know what they might be and cannot seem to find out."

Iris smiled at him as he stood there at a loss, rubbing his forehead with his hand.

"I always feel the same way," she said to Anselm in her light, birdlike voice, "whenever I smell a flower. My heart feels as though a memory of something completely beautiful and precious were bound up with the fragrance, something that was mine a long time ago and that I have lost.

It is that way too with music and sometimes with poems, suddenly there is a flash for an instant as though all at once I saw a lost homeland lying below in the valley, but instantly it is gone again and forgotten. I believe we are on earth for this purpose, for this contemplation and seeking and listening for lost, far-off strains, and behind them lies our true home."

"How beautifully you put it." he said admiringly, and he felt an almost painful stirring in his chest, as though a compass hidden there were persistently pointing towards his distant goal. But that goal was quite different from the one he had deliberately set for his life, which disturbed him. Was it, after all, worthy of him to squander his life in dreams with only pretty fairy tales for an excuse?

One day Anselm came back from one of his lonely journeys and found his barren scholar's quarters so chilly and oppressive that he rushed off to his friend's house, determined to ask Iris for her hand.

"Iris, I don't want to go on living this way. You have always been my good friend. I must tell you everything. I need a wife, otherwise my life seems empty and meaningless. And whom should I want for a wife but you, my darling flower? Are you willing? You shall have flowers, as many as we can find, you shall have the most beautiful garden. Are you willing to come to me?"

Iris looked him calmly in the eye with deliberation. She did not smile, she did not blush and she answered him with a firm voice. "Anselm, I am not surprised at your request. You are dear to me but I had never thought of being your wife."

"Look my friend," she continued, "I demand a great deal from the man I marry. I make more demands than most women. You offer me flowers and you mean well by it. But I can live without flowers, and without music too; I can very well do without many other things as well, if necessary.

The one thing I cannot and will not do without is that I can never live so much as a single day in such a way that the music in my heart is not playing.

If I am to live with a man, it must be one whose inner music harmonizes beautifully and exactly with mine and his single desire must be that his own music be pure and that it blends well with mine.

Can you do that, my friend? Very likely you will not become more famous this way or garner further honors, your house will be quiet, and the furrows which I have seen in your brow for many a year must all be smoothed out.

Oh, Anselm, it will not work. Look, you are so

constituted that you always have to study new furrows into your forehead, constantly create new worries. I have no doubt that you love me and that you find me pleasant, but I feel that what you are really after is simply a pretty toy.

Listen to me carefully, everything that now seems a toy to you is life itself to me and would have to be so to you too, and everything you strive for and worry about is for me a toy, in my eyes, it is not worth living for.

I will not change, Anselm, because I live according to an inner law, but will you be able to change? And you would have to change completely if I were to be your wife."

Anselm could not speak, startled by the strength of her will, which he had always thought weak and frivolous.

He remained silent and thoughtlessly crushed a flower he had picked up from the table in his nervous hand.

When Iris gently took the flower from him, her action struck him to the heart, like a sharp rebuke.

Suddenly she smiled cheerfully and charmingly, as though she had unexpectedly found a way out of the darkness.

"I have an idea," she said in a gentle voice, and blushed as she spoke. "You might find it strange, it might seem to you a whim. But it is not a whim. Will you listen to it? And will you agree that it decides about you and me?"

Without understanding, Anselm looked at Iris with worry in his pale features. Her smile compelled him to have confidence and say yes.

"I want to give you a task," Iris said, becoming immediately very serious again.

"Do so, it is your right," Anselm replied.

"This is serious." she said, "And it is my last word. Will you accept it as it comes straight from my soul and not quibble or bargain about it, even if you don't understand it right away?"

When Anselm promised, Iris got up, gave him her hand and said "You have often said to me that whenever you speak my name you are reminded of a forgotten something that was once important and holy in your eyes.

That is a sign, Anselm, and it is what has drawn you to me all these years. I too believe you have lost and forgotten something important and holy in your soul, something that must be reawakened before you can find happiness and attain what is intended for you.

Farewell, Anselm! I give you my hand and I beg you, go and make sure you find again in your memory what it is you are reminded of by my name. The day you rediscover that, I will go with you as your wife wherever you wish and have no desires but yours."

In confusion and dismay, Anselm tried to interrupt her and dismiss this demand as a whim, but with one bright look she reminded him of his promise and he fell silent. With lowered eyes he took her hand, raised it to his lips, and left.

In the course of his life he had taken upon himself many tasks and had carried them out, but none had been so strange, important, and at the same time dismaying as this one. Day after day he hurried around concentrating on it until he became weary.

Times always came when in despair and anger he denounced the whole undertaking as a crazy feminine notion and rejected it completely.

But then something deep within him disagreed, a very faint secret pain, a soft, scarcely audible warning. This low voice, which was in his own heart, acknowledged that Iris was right and it made the same demand that she did.

However, the task was much too difficult for this man of learning. He was supposed to remember something he had long ago forgotten, he was to find once more a single golden thread in the fabric of the sunken years.

He was to grasp with his hands and deliver to his beloved something that was no more than a vanished bird song, an impulse of joy or sorrow on hearing a piece of music, something finer, more fleeting and bodiless than a thought, more insubstantial than a dream, as formless as morning mist.

Sometimes when he had abandoned the search and given up in bad temper, unexpectedly something like a breath from a distant garden touched him, he whispered the name Iris to himself ten times and more, softly and lightly, like one testing a note on a tight string.

"Iris," he whispered, "Iris," and with a faint pain he felt something stir within him, the way in an old abandoned house a door swings open without reason or a cup-board creaks.

He went over his memories, which he believed to be stored away in good order, and made amazing and startling discoveries.

His treasury of memories was a great deal smaller than he had thought. Whole years were missing, and when he thought back they stood there as empty as blank pages.

He found that he had great difficulty in summoning up a clear image of his mother. He had completely forgotten the name of a girl whom as a youth he had hotly courted for a whole year.

He happened to remember a dog he had once purchased on the spur of the moment and had kept with him for a time; it took him a whole day to recall the dog's name.

Painfully, with increasing sorrow and fear, the poor fellow saw how wasted and empty was the life that lay behind him, no longer belonging to him, alien and with no relationship to himself, like something once learned by heart of which one could now only with difficulty retrieve meaningless fragments.

He began to write; he wanted to set down, going backward year by year, his most important experiences so as to have them clearly in mind again. But what had been his most important experiences?

When he was appointed professor? When he received his doctorate, been an undergraduate, been a secondary school student? Or when once in the forgotten past this girl or that had for a time pleased him?

He looked up terrified: Was this life? Was this all? He struck himself on the forehead and laughed bitterly.

Meanwhile, time ran on, never had it fled so inexorably! A year was gone and it seemed to him that he was in exactly the same position as when he had left Iris. Yet in this time he had greatly changed, as everyone except himself recognized.

He had become almost a stranger to his acquaintances, he was considered absent minded, peevish, and odd, he gained a reputation of being an unpredictable eccentric, too bad but he had been a bachelor for too long.

There were times when he forgot his academic duties and his students waited for him in vain. Deep in thought, he would sometimes prowl through the streets, brushing the house-fronts and the dust from the window sills with his threadbare coat as he passed.

Many thought that he started to drink. But at other times he would stop in the midst of a classroom lecture, attempting to recall something; his face would break into an appealing childlike smile in a manner entirely new to him, and then he would go on talking with a warmth of feeling that touched many of his listeners to the heart.

In the course of his hopeless search for some continuity among the faint traces of bygone years, he had acquired a new faculty of which he was not aware.

It happened more and more frequently that behind what he used to call memories there lay other memories, much like an old wall painted with ancient pictures still older ones have been over-painted and lie hidden and unsuspected.

He would try to recall something, perhaps the name of a city where he had once spent some days on his travels, or the birthday of a friend, or anything at all, and while he was burrowing and searching through a little piece of the past as though through rubble, suddenly something entirely different would occur to him. A breath would unexpectedly reach him like an April morning breeze or a September mist.

He smelled a fragrance, tasted a flavor, felt delicate dark sensations here and there, on his skin, in his eyes, in his heart, and slowly it came to him that there must once have been a day, blue and warm or cool and gray, or whatever kind of day, and the essence of it must have been caught within him and clung there as a buried memory.

He could not place in the real past that spring or winter day he distinctly smelled the fragrance or felt that certain way. He could not attach name or date to it. Perhaps it was during his college days, perhaps he was still in the cradle, but the fragrance was there and he knew that something lived in him which he did not recognize and could not identify or define.

Sometimes it seemed to him as though these memories might well reach back beyond life into a former existence and he would smile at the thought.

Anselm discovered a good deal in his helpless wanderings through the abyss of memory. He found much that touched and gripped him, and much that startled him and filled him with terror, but the one thing he did not find was what the name Iris meant to him.

In the torment of his fruitless search he went once to explore his old home, saw the woods and the streets, the footpaths and fences, stood in the old garden of his childhood and felt the waves break over his heart, the past engulfing him like a dream.

Saddened and silent, he returned and with the announcement that he was ill he had everyone who wanted to see him turned away.

One, however, insisted on entering, the friend he had not seen since his courtship of Iris had ended. His friend found him sitting unkempt in his cheerless study.

"Get up," he said to him, "and come with me. Iris wants to see you." Anselm sprang to his feet. "Iris! What has happened to her? — Oh, I know, I know!"

"Yes," said his friend, "come with me. She is dying. She has been ill for a long time."

They went to Iris. She was lying on a sofa, slender and light as a child. She smiled luminously with overlarge eyes and gave Anselm her pale white childlike hand, which lay like a flower in his. Her face was as though transfigured.

"Anselm," she said, "are you angry with me? I set you a hard task and I see that you have remained faithful. Go on searching, go on as you have been doing until you find what you are looking for. You thought you were searching on my account but you were doing it for yourself. Do you realize that?"

"I suspected it," Anselm said, "and now I know it. It is a vast journey, Iris, and I would long since have turned back, but now I can find no way to do that. I don't know what is to become of me."

She gazed deep into his sorrowful eyes and smiled encouragingly; he bent over her thin hand and wept in silence, and her hand became wet with his tears.

"What is to become of you?" she said in a voice that was only like a glow of memory.

"What is to become of you is something you must not ask. You have sought many things in your life.

You have sought honor and happiness and knowledge and you have sought me, your little Iris. All these were only pretty pictures and they deserted you, as I must now desert you.

It has been the same with me. What I sought always turned out to be dear and lovely pictures and they always failed and faded.

Now I have no more pictures, I seek nothing more, I am returning home and have only one small step to take and then I shall be in my native land. You too will join me there, Anselm, and then you will have no more furrows in your brow."

She was so pale that Anselm cried out in despair: "Oh, wait, Iris, do not go yet. Leave me some sign that you are not disappearing completely." She nodded and reached over to a vase beside her and gave him a fresh, full-blown blue sword lily.

"Here, take my flower, the iris, and do not forget me. Search for me, search for the iris, then you will come to me." Weeping, Anselm held the flower in his hands and took his leave.

When a message came from his friend, he returned and helped adorn Iris's coffin with flowers and lower it into the ground. Then his life fell to pieces. It seemed impossible for him to go on spinning his thread. He gave everything up, left his position and the city, and disappeared from the world.

He would turn up briefly here and there. He was seen in his native town leaning over the fence of the old flower garden, but when people inquired after him and wanted to assist him he was nowhere to be found.

The sword lily remained dear to him. Whenever he came upon one, he would bend over it and sink his gaze into its chalice for a long time and out of the bluish depths a fragrance and a memory of all that had been and was to be seemed to rise towards him, until sadly he went his way because fulfillment did not come.

It was as though he was listening at a half-open door and behind it the most enchanting secret was being breathed, and just when he felt that at that very moment everything would be made plain to him and would be fulfilled, the door would swing shut and the chill wind of the world would blow over his loneliness.

In his dreams his mother spoke to him. He had not seen her face and form so close and clear for many long years.

Iris spoke to him too. When he woke up, an echo lingered in his ears to which he would devote a whole day of thought.

He had no permanent residence. He hurried through the country like a stranger, slept in hostels or in the woods, ate bread or berries, drank wine or the dew from the leaves of bushes, but was oblivious to it all. Some took him for a fool, some for a magician, some feared him, some laughed at him, many loved him.

He acquired skills he had never had before, like being with children and taking part in their strange games, or holding conversations with a broken twig or a little stone.

Winters and summers raced by him, he kept looking into the chalices of flowers and into rivers and lakes. "Pictures, everything just pictures." he said at times to himself, but within him he felt an essence that was not a picture and this he followed, and the essence within him at times would speak, and its voice was the voice of Iris and the voice of his mother, and it was comfort and hope.

Wonders came his way but did not surprise him. One winter day he was walking through the snow in an open field, ice forming in his beard.

There in the snow stood slim and pointed an iris stalk which bore a single beautiful blossom. He bent over to it and smiled, for now he realized what it was that Iris had again and again urged him to remember.

He recognized his childhood dream when he saw between the golden pickets the light-blue, brightly veined path leading into the secret heart of the flower. He knew that this was what he sought, that this was the essence and not any longer a picture. Premonitions came to him again and dreams guided him.

He found a hut where children gave him milk, and as he played with them they told him stories. They told him that in the forest near the charcoal burners' huts a miracle had occurred. There the spirit gate had been seen standing open, the gate that opens only once in a thousand years.

He listened and nodded assent to the cherished picture and went on. A bird in an alder bush sang in front of him. It sang with a strange sweet note like the voice of the dead Iris.

He followed the bird as it flew and hopped ahead of him, deep into the forest. When the bird fell silent and disappeared, Anselm stopped and looked about him.

He was standing in a deep valley in the forest where water ran softly under broad green leaves. All was silent as if full of expectation.

In Anselm's heart the bird continued to sing with an angelic voice and it urged him on until he stood in front of a cliff overgrown with moss, and in the middle of it was a gaping fissure cave that led narrowly into the interior of the mountain.

An old man sat in front of the cave. He stood up when he saw Anselm approaching and shouted "You there, turn back! This is the spirit gate. No one has ever returned who entered here."

Anselm looked up and into the rocky entrance. There he saw a blue path disappearing deep inside the mountain with golden pillars standing close together on both sides. The path led downward as though into an enormous flower chalice.

In Anselm's heart rose the bird's clear song and he walked past the guardian and into the fissure and between the golden columns into the blue mystery of the interior. It was Iris into whose heart he entered, and it was the sword lily in his mother's garden into whose blue chalice he softly strode. As he silently drew closer to the golden twilight, all memory and all knowledge were suddenly at his command.

He felt his hand and found it small and soft, voices of love sounded near and familiar in his ears, and the ring they had and the glow of the golden columns were like the ring and glow everything had at that distant time in the springtime of his childhood.

The dream he had dreamed as a small boy was his again, that he was striding into the chalice, and behind him the whole world of images strode too and glided and sank into the mystery that lies behind all images. Softly Anselm began to sing, and his path sloped gently downward into his homeland.

Hermann Hesse

Fine Dream Sequence

Nothing attracted or held my attention in that stuffy saloon except the presence of this beautiful young lady who looked like a classy hooker. I longed in vain to get just one good look at her face but it kept on floating dimly amid loose dark hair like a cloud of sweet milky whiteness.

Her eyes were probably dark brown, I felt some inner reason to expect that. But if they were then her eyes wouldn't match the face I was trying to read into. That indeterminate pallor whose shape I knew lay buried in deep inaccessible levels of my memory.

I slowly diverted my gaze to the northern window where a false sea and an imitation fjord shown through. I was getting rather bored and I felt like I have spent a vast amount of tedious and unprofitable time in that saloon. Finally something happened.

Two young men entered the saloon. They greeted the lady with elaborate courtesy and were introduced to me.

"Monkeys", I thought and was annoyed at myself because the pretty stylish cut and fit of the reddish-brown jacket one of them was wearing filled me with envy. A horrible feeling of envy towards an irreproachable man with an unabashed smile!

"Pull yourself together!" I commanded inwardly.

The two young men reached indifferently for my extended hand, why did I offer it? They were wearing derisive smiles which made me realize that something was wrong with me.

I felt a disturbing chill creeping up my legs, as I looked down I grew pale when I saw that I stood shoeless with only socks on my feet.

Again and again these shabby, miserable, sordid frustrations and disadvantages! They never happen to others, that they appear naked or half naked in saloons before the company of the irreproachably correct!

Disheartened, I tried at least to conceal my left foot with my right. As I did, my eyes strayed through the window and I saw the steep wild blue ocean cliffs threatening with false and sinister colors and demonic intent.

Worried and seeking help, I looked at the two strangers, full of hatred for them and full of greater hatred for myself. Nothing turned out right for me, that was the trouble. And why did I feel responsible for that stupid sea? Well, if that was the way I felt, then I was responsible.

I looked the man in the reddish-brown jacket eagerly in the face. His cheeks shone with health and careful grooming, and I knew perfectly well that I was exposing myself to no purpose, that he couldn't be influenced.

At that moment he noticed my feet in their coarse dark-green socks and smiled disagreeably. Oh, I could still be thankful there were no holes in them. He nudged his friend and pointed at my feet. His friend, too, grinned in derision.

"Just look at the sea!" I shouted, gesturing towards the window.

The man in the reddish-brown jacket shrugged his shoulders. It did not occur to him to so much as turn towards the window.

He then said something to his friend which I only half understood, but it was aimed at me and had to do with fellows with socks on their feet who really shouldn't be tolerated in such a saloon. As I listened, the word "saloon" had for me, as it had in my childhood, the half-seductive half-meretricious ring of worldly distinction.

Close to tears, I bent over to see whether anything could be done about my feet, and now perceived that they had slipped out of loose house shoes; a very big soft dark-red bedroom slipper lay behind me on the floor. I took the slipper in my hand uncertainly, holding it by the heel, still strongly inclined to weep. It slipped away from me, I caught it as it fell. Meanwhile, it had grown even larger and, now, I held it by the toe.

All at once I had a feeling of inner release and realized the great value of the slipper, which was vibrating a little in my hand, weighted down by its heavy heel. How splendid to have such a limp red shoe, so soft and heavy! Experimentally I swung it a few times through the air, this was delicious and flooded me with ecstasy to the roots of my hair.

A club or a blackjack were nothing in comparison with my great shoe. Calziglione was the Italian name I called it. When I gave the man in the reddish-brown jacket a playful blow on the head with the Calziglione, the young irreproachable fell reeling to the chair, and the others and the room and the dreadful sea lost all their power over me.

I was big and strong. I was free. As I gave the man in the reddish-brown jacket a second blow on the head with the Calziglione, there was no longer any contest, there was no more need for demeaning self-defense in my actions but simple exaltation and free lordly whim.

Now, I did not hate my vanquished foe in the least. On the contrary, I found him interesting. He was precious and dear to me, after all I was his master and his creator.

For every good blow of my Calziglione that primitive and ape-like head was forged, rebuilt and reformed. With every constructive impact it grew more attractive, handsomer, finer, became my creature and my work, a thing that satisfied me and that I loved.

With a final expert blacksmith's blow I flattened the pointed occiput just enough. He was finished. He thanked me and stroked my hand.

"It's all right." I said, waving to him.

He crossed his hands over his chest and said eagerly: "My name is Paul." My chest swelled with a marvelous feeling of power, a feeling that expanded the space about me; the room — no more talk of "saloon"! — shriveled with shame and crept emptily away.

I stood beside the sea which turned blue-black with steel clouds pressing down upon the sombre mountains. Dark water boiled up in the fjord with foaming storm squalls straying in circles; compulsive, terrifying.

I looked up and raised my hand to signal that the storm could begin. A bolt of lightning bright and cold exploded out of the harsh blue and a warm typhoon descended howling. Tumultuous gray forms streamed apart in the heavens like veined marble.

Humpbacked waves rose terrifyingly from the tormented sea and the storm tore sprays from their tops and stinging wisps of foam and whipped them in my face. The indifferent black mountains tore open eyes full of horror. Their silent cowering together rang out like a humble prayer.

In the midst of the magnificent charge of the storm, mounted on gigantic ghostly horses, a timid voice spoke close to me. Oh, I had not forgotten you, pale lady of the long black hair. I bent over to her and she spoke to me childishly "The sea is coming, one could not stay there."

I was touched and continued to look at the gentle sinner, her face was only a quiet pallor amid the encircling twilight of her hair, then the chiding waves were already striking at my knees and at my chest, and the woman floated helpless and silent on the rising waters.

I laughed a little, put my arm under her knees, and raised her up to me. This too was beautiful and liberating.

The woman was strangely light and small and full of fresh warmth. Her eyes were sincere, trusting, and alarmed.

I saw that she was not a prostitute at all, not even a distant or incomprehensible woman. No sins, no mystery; she was just a child.

Out of the waves and across the rocks I carried her through the rain-darkened royally grieving park to where the storm could not reach.

From the bowed crowns of ancient trees simple soft human beauty spoke pure poems and symphonies; a world of noble intimations and charmingly civilized delights.

Enchanting trees painted by Corot and noble rustic woodwind music by Schubert subtly tempted me to the beloved temple in a momentary upsurge of nostalgia. But in vain; the world has many voices, and the soul has its hours and its moments for everything.

Only God knows how the sinner, the pale woman, the child, took her leave and disappeared from sight.

There was an outside stairway of stone, there was an entrance gate, there were servants present, all dim and cloudy as though behind translucent glass.

There was something else even more insubstantial, even more cloudy, figures blown there by the wind. A note of censure and reproach directed against me aroused my ire at that storm of shadows.

All disappeared except the form of Paul, my friend and son Paul, and in his features was revealed and hidden an infinitely familiar, yet unnamable, face. The face of a school-mate, the primeval legendary face of a nursemaid, composed of the good nourishing half-memories of the fabulous earliest years.

Good heart-comforting darkness, warm cradle of the soul and lost homeland, opens before me the time of embryonic being, the first uncertain quivering above the fountain's source, beneath which, sleep ancient times with their dreams of tropical forests.

Do but feel your way soul, do but wander, plunge blindly into the rich bath of guiltless twilight desires! I know you, timid soul, nothing is more necessary to you, nothing is so much food, drink, and sleep for you, as the return to your beginnings.

There the waves roar around you and you are a wave, the forest rustles and you are the forest. There is no outer and no inner any more. You fly, a bird in the air, you swim, a fish in the sea, you breathe in light and are light, taste darkness and are darkness.

We wander, soul, we swim and fly and smile and, with delicate ghostly fingers, we retie the torn filaments and blissfully unite the disjointed harmonies. We no longer seek God. We are God.

We are the world. We kill and die along with others, we create and are resurrected with our dreams.

Our finest dream, that is the blue sky, our finest dream, that is the sea, our finest dream, that is the starlit night, and is the fish and is the bright happy light and bright happy sounds. Everything is our dream, each is our finest dream.

We have just died and become earth. We have just discovered laughter. We have just arranged a constellation. Voices resound and each is the voice of our mother. Trees rustle, and each one of them rustles above our cradle. Roads diverge in a star pattern and each road leads towards home.

The one who had called himself Paul, my creature and my friend, was there again and had become as old as I was. He resembled a friend of my youth, but I did not know which one and therefore I was a little uneasy with him and showed him a certain courtesy. From this he drew power.

The world no longer obeyed me, it obeyed him and therefore everything that had preceded had disappeared, collapsed in craven improbability. Put to shame by him who governed now.

We were in a square, the place was called Paris, and in front of me a steel beam towered into the air. It was a ladder and on both sides were small iron rungs to which one could hold with one's hands and on which one could climb with one's feet.

Since Paul desired it, I climbed first with him beside me on an identical ladder. When we had climbed as high as a house or a very high tree, I began to feel frightened.

I looked over at Paul, he felt no fear but he recognized my own and smiled. For the space of a breath while he smiled and I stared at him, I was very close to recognizing his face and remembering his name.

A fissure in the past opened and split down to my school days, back to the time when I was twelve years old, life's most glorious period when everything was full of fragrance, every-thing was congenial, everything was gilded with an edible smell of fresh bread and an intoxicating shimmer of adventure.

Jesus was twelve years old when he shamed the scribes in the temple. At twelve we have all shamed our scribes and teachers, have been smarter than they, more gifted than they, braver than they.

Memories and images pressed in upon me. Forgotten schoolbooks, detention during the noon hour, a bird killed with a slingshot, a coat pocket stickily filled with stolen plums, wild, boyish splashing in the swimming pool.

Torn Sunday trousers and torments of conscience, ardent prayers at night about earthly problems, marvelous heroic feelings of magnificence on reading verses by Schiller.

It was only a second's lightning flash, avidly hurrying picture sequences without focus. In the next instant Paul's face stared at me again, tormentingly half recognized. I was no longer sure of my age, possibly we were boys.

Farther and farther below the narrow rungs of our ladders lay the mass of streets that was called Paris. When we were higher than any tower, our steel beams came to an end and proved to be surmounted, each of them, by a horizontal board, a minuscule platform. It seemed impossible to get on top of these. But Paul did it negligently and I had to do it too.

Once on top I laid myself flat on the board and looked down over the edge as though from a high little cloud. My glance fell like a stone into emptiness and found no goal. Then my friend pointed with his hand and I became fascinated by a marvelous sight that hovered in mid-air.

There, above a broad avenue at the level of the highest roofs but immensely far below us, I saw a foreign-looking company; they seemed to be high-wire dancers and indeed one of the figures was running to and fro on a wire or rod.

Then I discovered that there were a great many of them, almost all young girls, and they seemed to me to be gypsies or other nomadic folk.

They walked, lay, sat, moved at the height of the

roofs on an airy framework of the thinnest scaffolding and wooden poles, they lived there and were at home in that region.

Beneath them the street could only be imagined, a fine swirling mist extending from the ground up almost to their feet. Paul made some remark about it.

"Yes," I replied, "it is pathetic, all those girls."

To be sure, I was much higher than they were, but I was clinging to my position and they moved lightly and fearlessly, and I saw that I was too high, I was in the wrong place.

They were at the right height, not on the ground and yet not so devilishly high and distant as I was, not among people and yet not so completely isolated; moreover, there were many of them.

I saw very well that they represented a bliss that I had not yet attained.

But I knew that sooner or later I would have to climb down my monstrous ladder and the thought of it was so oppressive that I felt nauseated and could not endure being up there for another instant.

Desperate and shaking with dizziness, I felt beneath me with my feet for the rungs of the ladder — I could not see them from the board — and for hideous minutes hung at that terrifying height struggling convulsively.

No one helped me, Paul was gone. In abject fear I executed hazardous kicks and grasps, and a feeling came over me like a fog, a feeling that it was not the high ladder or the dizziness that I had to endure and taste to the full. For almost at once I lost the sight and form of things, everything turned to fog and confusion.

At one moment I was still hanging dizzily from the rungs, at the next I was creeping, small and frightened, through narrow underground passages and corridors, then I was wading hopelessly through mud and dung, feeling the filthy slime rising towards my mouth.

Darkness and obstacles were everywhere. Dreadful tasks of grave but shrouded significance. Fear and sweat, paralysis and cold. Hard death, hard birth. What endless night surrounded us! How many paths of torment we pursue, go deep into the cavern of our rubble-filled soul, eternal suffering hero, eternal Odysseus!

But we go on, we go on, we bow ourselves and wade, we swim, choking in the slime, we creep along smooth noxious walls. We weep and despair, we whimper in fear and howl aloud in pain. But we go on we go on and suffer, we go on and gnaw our way through.

Out of the seething hellish vapors visibility returned once more, a short stretch of the dark path was again revealed in the formative light of memory, and the soul forced its way out of the primeval world into the familiar circle of known time.

Where was this? Familiar objects gazed at me, I breathed an atmosphere I recognized. A big room in half darkness, a kerosene lamp on the table, my own lamp, a big round table rather like a piano.

My sister was there, and my brother-in-law, perhaps on a visit to me or perhaps I was with them. They were quiet and worried, full of concern about me. I stood in the big dim room, walked back and forth, stopped and walked again in a cloud of sadness, in a flood of bitter, choking sadness.

Now I began to look for something, nothing important, a book or a pair of scissors or something of that sort, and I could not find it. I took the lamp in my hand, it was heavy, and I was terribly weary, I soon put it down but then picked it up again and wanted to go on searching.

Searching! I knew it was useless. I would find nothing. I would only increase confusion everywhere, the lamp would fall from my hands, it was so heavy, so painfully heavy, and I would go on groping and searching and wandering through the room all my miserable long life.

My brother-in-law looked at me, worried and a little reproachful. They could see that I was going mad. I thought immediately, and picked up the lamp again. My sister came to me, silent with pleading eyes, full of fear and love, so that I felt my heart would break.

I could say nothing, I could only stretch out my hand and wave her off, motion to her to stay away, and I thought: Just leave me alone! Just leave me alone! You cannot know how I feel, how I suffer, how frightfully I suffer! And again: Leave me alone! Just leave me alone!

The reddish lamplight dimly flooded the big room, outside the trees groaned in the wind. For an instant I seemed to have a most profound inward vision and sensation of the night outside. Wind and wetness, autumn, the bitter smell of wet leaves. Fluttering leaves from the elm tree, autumn, autumn!

Once more, and for an instant, I was not myself but saw myself as though in a picture. I was a pale haggard musician with flickering eyes named Hugo Wolf and on this evening I was in the process of going mad.

Meanwhile, I had to go on searching, hopelessly searching, and lifting the heavy lamp on to the table, on to the chair, on to the bookcase.

I had to defend myself with pleading gestures when my sister once more looked at me sadly and considerately, wanting to comfort me, wanting to be near me and help me.

The sorrow within me grew and filled me to the

bursting point, and the images around me were of eloquent, engrossing quality, much clearer than any ordinary reality.

A few autumn flowers in a glass, with a dark reddish-brown mat beneath it, glowed with painfully beautiful loneliness. Everything, even the shining brass base of the lamp, was of an enchanted beauty and isolated by fateful separateness, as in the paintings of the great masters.

I saw my fate clearly. One deeper shade in this sadness, one further glance from my sister, one more look from the flowers, the beautiful soulful flowers, and the flood would come. I would sink into madness.

"Leave me! You do not understand!"

On the polished side of the piano a beam of lamplight was reflected in the dark wood, so beautiful, so mysterious, so filled with melancholy!

My sister rose again and went to the piano. I wanted to plead with her, I wanted to stop her by mental power but I could not, some sort of strength went out to her from my loneliness.

Oh, I knew what was certain to happen then. I knew the melody that would now inevitably find voice, saying all and destroying all.

Monstrous tension compressed my heart, and while the first burning tears sprang from my eyes, I threw my head and hands across the table and listened. With all my senses, and with newly added senses as well, I absorbed the words and the melody at once; Wolf's melody and the verses.

What do you know, dark treetops, of the beauty of olden times? The homeland beyond the mountains, How far from us now, how far!

At this, before my eyes and within me, the world slid apart, was swallowed up in tears and tones. Impossible to express the fluidity, the torrent, the beneficence and pain! O tears, O sweet collapse, blissfully melting away!

All the books of the world full of thoughts and poems are nothing in comparison with one minute's sobbing when feeling surges in waves. The soul perceives and finds itself in the depths. Tears are the melting ice of the soul, all angels are close to one who weeps.

Forgetful of all causes and reasons, I wept my way down from the heights of unbearable tension into the gentle twilight of ordinary feelings, without thoughts, without witnesses. In between, images fluttered: a coffin in which lay a man very dear and important to me, but I knew not who. Perhaps me myself, I thought.

Then another scene appeared to me from the far pale distance. Had I not years ago or in an earlier life witnessed a marvelous sight: a company of young girls living high in the air, cloud-like and weightless, beautiful and blissful, floating light as air and rich as string music?

Years flew between, forcing me gently but irresistibly away from the picture. Alas, perhaps my whole life had only this meaning, to see those lovely hovering maidens, to approach them, to become like them! Now they disappeared in the distance, unreachable, not understood and unreleased. Wearily encircled by fluttering desire and despair.

Years drifted down like snowflakes and the world was changed. I was wandering sadly towards a small house. I felt wretched, and an alarming sensation in my mouth preoccupied me, cautiously I poked my tongue at a doubtful tooth, which at once slipped sideways and fell out. The next one, it too!

I appealed to a very young doctor who was there, holding out one tooth in my fingers imploringly. He laughed merrily, dismissing me with a deadly professional glance and shaking his young head: "That doesn't amount to a thing, quite harmless, happens every day."

Dear God, I thought. But he went on and pointed at my left knee: "That's where the trouble was, that was something quite different and no joking matter."

With panic speed I reached down to my knee. There it was! There was a hole into which I could thrust my finger, and instead of skin and flesh there was nothing to feel but an insensitive, soft, spongy mass, light and fibrous as the substance of wilted plants. O my God, this was destruction, this was death and disintegration!

"So there's nothing more to be done?" I asked with painstaking friendliness. "Nothing more." said the young doctor and disappeared.

Exhausted, I walked towards the little house, not as desperate as I really should have been, in fact almost indifferent. Now I had to enter the little house where my mother was waiting for me. Had I not already heard her voice? Seen her face?

Steps led upward, crazy steps, high and smooth, without a railing, each one a mountain, each a summit, a glacier. It was certainly too late. Perhaps she had already left, perhaps she was already dead? Had I not just heard her call again?

Silently I struggled with the steep mountainous steps; falling and crushed, wild and sobbing, I climbed and strained, supporting myself on failing arms and knees, and was on top, was at the gate, and the steps were again small and pretty and bordered by boxwood.

My every stride was sluggish and heavy as though through slime and glue, no getting on, the gate stood open, and within, wearing a gray dress, my mother walked, a little basket on her arm, silently sunk in thought, her dark, slightly graying hair in the little net!

And her walk, the small figure! And the dress, the gray dress. Had I completely lost her image? For all those many many years, had I never properly thought of her at all?

There she was, there she stood and walked, only visible from behind, exactly as she always was, very clear and beautiful, pure love, pure thoughts of love!

Furiously I waded through the sticky air with paralyzed gait, tendrils of plants curled round me like thin strong ropes tighter and tighter, malignant obstacles everywhere, no getting on!

"Mother!" I cried. But I had no voice ... No sound came. There was glass between her and me. My mother walked on slowly without looking back, silently involved in beautiful loving thoughts, brushing with her familiar hand an invisible thread from her dress, bending over her little basket with her sewing materials. Oh, that little basket! In it she had once hidden an Easter egg for me. I cried out desperate and voiceless.

I ran but could not leave the spot! Tenderness and rage consumed me. And she walked on slowly through the summer house, stood in the open doorway on the other side, then stepped out into the open.

She let her head sink a little to one side, gently listening, absorbed in thoughts, raised and lowered the little basket. I remembered a slip of paper I had found as a boy in her sewing basket, on which she wrote in her flowing hand what she planned to do and take care of that day. "Put away laundry - iron Hermann's trousers — borrow book by Dickens — yesterday Hermann did not say his prayers." Rivers of memory, cargoes of love!

Bound and chained, I stood at the gate, and beyond it the woman in the gray dress walked slowly away, into the garden, and disappeared.

A Difficult Path

I stood hesitating at the dark entrance to the gorge on the top of the cliff and turned to look back. The sun was shining above the meadows, the grass flickered in a pleasant sea of green and the flowers waved.

It felt good to be out there in the warmth where one's soul hummed deep with satisfied and well-loved ease like a hairy bumblebee in the heavy fragrance and light.

I was probably a fool to want to leave all this and climb up into the mountain range. My guide touched me gently on the arm. I tore my eyes away from the lovely landscape, the way a man forcibly frees himself from a warm bath.

I saw the gorge lying ahead of me in sunless darkness, a little black stream crept out of the cliff and pale green grass grew in small tufts on its bank. Stones of all shades lay in the stream's bed, pale and dead like the bones of creatures that had tumbled there and died long ago.

"We'll take a rest," I said to the guide. He smiled indulgently and we sat down. Out of the rocky entrance flowed a gentle stream of dark stone-cold air. Nasty, nasty to go this way! Nasty to force oneself through this cheerless rocky entrance, to stride across this cold stream and to climb up in darkness into this narrow ragged gorge!

"The way looks horrible," I said in hesitation. As though from the dying embers of a fire, a strong unbelievable unreasoning hope flared up within me, the hope that we could perhaps still turn back, that my guide might allow himself to be persuaded, that we might be spared all this.

Yes, why not, really? Wasn't it a thousand times more beautiful in the place that we've just left? Didn't life there flow richer, warmer and more enchanting? Wasn't I a human being, a childlike short-lived creature with a right to some share of happiness, to a cozy corner in the sun, to the sight of blue sky and flowers?

I wanted to stay where I was. I had no wish to play the hero and martyr! I would be content all my life if I was allowed to stay in the valley and in the sun. I was already beginning to shiver. It was impossible to linger there for long.

"You're shivering. We better move on." My guide said as he stood up, stretched to his full height and looked down at me with a smile. There was neither derision nor sympathy in his smile, neither harshness nor compassion. There was nothing there but understanding, nothing but knowledge.

His smile said to me: "I know you. I know your fear and how you feel. I haven't forgotten your boasting yesterday and the day before. Every rabbity dodge of cowardice your soul is now indulging in and every flirty glance at the lovely sunshine out there is familiar and well known to me before you even act it out."

With this smile the guide looked at me and took the first stride into the dark rocky chasm ahead of us. I hated him and loved him as a condemned man hates and loves the ax above his neck.

I hated and despised his knowledge, his leadership, his calmness and his lack of amiable weaknesses. Above all, I hated everything in myself that agreed with him, that approved him, that wanted to be like him and to follow him.

He took a number of steps, walking on the stones through the dark stream and was just about to disappear from sight around the first bend.

"Stop!" I cried, so full of fear that I was compelled to think at the same time: If this was a dream then at this very moment my terror would dissolve it and I would wake up. "Stop!" I cried. "I cannot do it. I am not yet ready."

The guide stopped and looked at me in silence, without reproach but with that dreadful understanding of his. That unbearable knowledge that he has completely understood all that is happening to me, in advance.

"Would you rather that we turn back?" he asked

He had not yet finished saying the last word when I knew, full of rebellion, that I would say no, that I would have to say no. Yet, at the same time, everything long familiar, loved, and trusted within me cried in desperation: "Say yes, say yes!"

The whole world and my homeland were chained like an iron ball to my leg. I wanted to shout yes but knew very well that I could not do it.

With outstretched arm the guide pointed back into the valley and I turned around once more towards that well-loved landscape. What I saw then was the most painful thing that could have happened to me.

I saw my beloved valleys and fields lying dull and pale under a weak white sun, the colors clashed false and shrill and the shadows, rusty black and without magic. The heart was cut out of everything, everything. The charm and fragrance were gone and everything smelled and tasted of over-indulgence to the point of nausea.

Oh, how well I knew all this. How I hated and feared this horrid trick of the guide, this degradation of what was dear and pleasant to me, causing the sap and spirit to drain out of it, falsifying the smells and poisoning the colors!

Oh, how well I knew all this. What was wine but yesterday, today was vinegar. And the vinegar would never become wine again. Never again. Silent and sad, I followed the guide.

He was right of course, now as always. It was a good thing at least that he remained visible instead of, as so often happened at moments of decision, disappearing suddenly and leaving me alone. Alone with that alien voice inside my head into which at such times he transformed himself. I was silent but my heart cried passionately: "Stay, stay, I will surely follow!"

The stones in the stream were slippery as hell and it was tiring and dizzying to walk like this, step by step on narrow wet stones that slipped away and shrank under one's feet.

The path in the stream began to rise steeply and the dark cliff walls drew closer together. They swelled ominously and every corner showed the malicious intention of clamping down behind us and cutting off our retreat forever.

Following my guide, I walked and walked over wart-covered yellow rocks with viscous slimy sheets of water. There was no sky above our heads, neither blue nor cloudy. I often closed my eyes in fear and disgust.

I saw a dark flower growing beside the path, velvety black with an air of sadness. It was beautiful and spoke to me as if it knew me, but my guide walked faster. I felt that if I lingered for a single moment, if I confer so much as one more glance on that sad velvety eye, then my depression and hopeless gloom would become over-whelming and unendurable. That my spirit would remain forever imprisoned in that mocking region of senseless and madness.

Wet and dirty, I crept on. As the damp walls came closer together above us my guide began to sing his old chant of consolation. In his strong clear youthful voice he sang in time to each stride: "I will, I will, I will!"

I knew very well that he wanted to encourage me and spur me on. He wanted to divert me from the hideous toil and hopelessness of this hellish journey. I knew that he was waiting for me to chime in with his singsong. But I refused to do it. I would not grant him that victory.

Was I in any mood to sing? Wasn't I a human being, a poor simple fellow who in defiance of his own heart had been drawn into situations and deeds which he could not expect? Were not every forget-me-not and every pink flower allowed to stay where it grew along the stream. To bloom and wither after its own fashion?

"I will, I will, I will!" the guide sang uninterruptedly. If only I were able to turn back! But with my guide's skilful help I had long since clambered over walls and abysses across which there was no possible return.

Tears burned in my throat but I dared not weep, so I defiantly and loudly joined in the guide's song, in the same rhythm and tone but not with his words; instead I sang "I must, I must, I must!"

It was not easy to sing and climb at the same time and soon I lost my breath and, gasping for air, I was forced to fall silent. But he went on singing unwearied: "I will, I will, I will," and in time he compelled me after all to join in singing his words.

The climbing got easier and I no longer felt under compulsion to continue. In fact I wished to go on. As for weariness from singing, there was no further trace of that. Then there was a brightness inside me and, as it increased, the smooth cliff receded too and became drier and became kinder which helped with my ever slipping feet. Above all more and more of the clear blue sky appeared, like a little blue stream between rocky banks, and then like a little blue lake that grew longer and wider.

I tried to exert my will more intensely and more profoundly, and the heavenly lake continued to grow and the path became more climbable. At times, I hurried over long stretches easily keeping pace with my guide.

Then, out of the blue, I saw the summit close above us. Steep and glittering in the shining sunny air. We crawled out of the narrow crevasse a short distance below the summit as the sun assailed my dazzled eyes.

When I opened my eyes again my knees shook with dread as I found myself standing free and without support on a sheer ridge. All around me there were infinite space and terrifying blue depths.

The narrow summit towered above us thin as a ladder. The sky and sun were there once more as we climbed up that last terrifying pitch, step by step, with compressed lips and knotted brows.

We stood on the summit, trivial figures on the sun-warmed rock in the sharp bitingly thin air. That was a strange mountain and a strange summit! We had reached the top by climbing over completely naked walls of stone.

A short sturdy tree with several powerful branches grew out of the stones above the summit. It stood hard and unyielding in the rock, inconceivably lonely and strange with the cool blue of heaven between its branches.

A black bird sat singing at the top of the tree. Its harsh song implied "Eternity, Eternity!"

The sun blazed, the rock glowed, the tree rose unyielding and the bird sang harshly. Quiet a dream of brief repose above the world!

The blackbird sang, and its blank hard eye stared at us like a black crystal. Its gaze was hard to bear and its song was hard to bear.

The loneliness and emptiness of that place, the expanse of the barren heavens, were frightful.

To die was an inconceivable bliss, to stay there was a nameless pain. Something must happen at once, instantly, otherwise, we and the world would turn to stone from sheer horror.

I felt the event drifting towards us, hot and oppressive, like a puff of wind before a storm. I felt it flickering over my body and soul like a burning fever. It threatened, it was coming, it was there.

Suddenly the bird whirled from the tree and plunged head-long into space. With a leap my guide dived into the blue and fell towards the flashing heavens. He flew away!

Now the wave of fate had reached its peak. It tore away my heart and then broke in silence. I was falling already.

I plunged, leaped, I flew. Wrapped in a cold vortex, I shot, blissful and palpitating with ecstatic pain, down through infinity, back to the mother's breast.

Hermann Hesse

The Poet

As he entered his teenage years, Han Fook became animated by an intense desire to become a poet and to perfect the art of poetry. In those days, Han was still living in his home city on the Yellow river in northern China. A handsome young man, he was modest, cheerful and of agreeable manners.

Despite his youth, Han had a solid education and was already known among the literary crowd in his district for a number of remarkable poems.

He has just got engaged, at his own wish and with the help of his parents who loved him dearly, to a young woman from a good family and the wedding was about be announced on a chosen day of good omen.

Han was not exactly rich but he had the expectation of comfortable means, which would be increased by the dowry of his bride.

Since his wife-to-be was both virtuous and beautiful, nothing seemed lacking to his future happiness. Nevertheless, Han was not entirely content, for his heart was filled with the ambition to become a perfect poet.

One evening, when a lantern festival was being celebrated on the river, Han was wandering alone on the opposite side. As he leaned against a tree that hung out over the water, he saw a thousand lights, floating and trembling, mirrored in the river.

He saw men, women and young girls on boats and barges, greeting each other and glowing, in their festive robes, like beautiful flowers.

89

He heard young women singing, the gentle weepings of guitars and the sweet tones of the flute players. Above all this he saw the bluish night arched like the dome of a temple.

Young Han's heart beat high as he took in all this beauty, a lonely observer in pursuit of his whim.

Much as he longed to go across the river and take part in the feast and be in the company of his bride-to-be and his friends, deep inside he longed to absorb it all as a perceptive observer and to reproduce it in a wholly perfect poem.

The blue of the night and the play of light on the water and the joy of the guests and the yearning of the silent onlooker leaning against a tree trunk on the bank of a river.

Han realized that at all festivals and with all joys of this earth he would never feel wholly comfortable and serene at heart; even in the midst of life he would remain solitary and would be, to a certain extent, a watcher, an alien.

He felt that his soul, unlike most others, was so formed that he must be alone to experience both the beauty of the earth and the secret longings of a stranger.

Han felt sad, pondered this matter but concluded that true happiness and deep satisfaction could only be his if he succeeds in mirroring the world so perfectly in his poems that in these mirror images he would possess the essence of the world, purified, eternal.

Han hardly knew whether he was still awake or had fallen asleep when he heard a slight rustling and saw a stranger standing beside the tree, a respectable old man wearing a violet robe.

Han roused himself and greeted the stranger with a salutation appropriate to the aged and distinguished.

The stranger smiled and spoke a few verses in which everything the young man had just felt was expressed so completely and beautifully and so exactly in accord with the rules of the great poets.

The young man's heart stood still with amazement "Who are you?" he cried. He bowed deeply and continued "You seem to be able to see into my soul and to recite more beautiful verses than I have ever heard from any of my teachers!"

The stranger smiled and said: "If you wish to be a poet, come to me. You will find my hut beside the source of this Great River in the north-western mountains. I am called Master of the Perfect Word."

Then the aged man stepped into the narrow shadow of the tree and instantly disappeared.

Han searched for him in vain but found no trace. Finally, he decided that the whole thing was a dream, probably caused by his fatigue.

Han crossed the river in a boat and joined the festival. Between the conversations and the music of the flutes he continued to hear the mysterious voice of the stranger.

His soul seemed to have gone away with the old man, for he sat remote and with dreaming eyes among the merry folk, who teased him for being in love.

A few days later, when Han's father was about to call friends and family to decide on the perfect day for the wedding, Han demurred and said:

"Forgive me if I seem to offend against the duty a son owes his father. But you know how deep my longing to distinguish myself in the art of poetry.

Even though some of my friends praise my poems, I very well know that I am still a beginner in the art and still on the first stage of the journey.

That is why I beg you to let me go my own way

alone for a while and devote myself to my studies. I honestly think having a wife and a house to take care of will keep me from achieving my goal.

I am still young and without other duties and would like to live for a time for my poetry, from which I hope to gain joy and fame."

Han's speech filled his father with surprise and he said:

"This art must indeed be dearer to you than anything, since you wish to postpone your wedding on account of it. Or has something happened between you and your bride?

If so, let me know and I can help to reconcile you, or select another girl."

The son swore that his bride-to-be was no less dear to him than she had been yesterday and always, and that no shadow of discord had fallen between them.

Then he told his father that on the day of the lantern festival a Master came to him in a dream, and that he desired to be his pupil more ardently than all the happiness in the world.

"Very well," said his father, "I will grant you a year. In this time you may pursue your dream, which perhaps was sent to you by a god."

"It may even take two years," said Han hesitantly. "Who can tell?"

So his father let him go but was troubled and the youth wrote a letter to his bride, bid farewell, and departed.

Han wandered for a long time till he reached the source of the river. In complete isolation he found a bamboo hut. In front of the hut, on a woven mat, sat the aged man whom he had seen beside the tree on the river bank.

The man sat playing a lute, and when he saw his

guest approach with reverence he did not rise or greet him but simply smiled and let his delicate fingers run over the strings.

A magical music flowed like a silver cloud through the valley and Han stood amazed. In his sweet astonishment he forgot everything.

When the Master of the Perfect Word laid aside his little lute and stepped into the hut, Han followed him reverently and stayed with him as his servant and pupil.

Within a month he learned to despise all the poems he had ever composed and he erased them out of his memory.

Within few more months, he erased all the songs that he had learned from his teachers at home.

The Master rarely spoke to him; in silence he taught him the art of lute playing until the pupil's being was entirely saturated with music.

Once Han made a little poem which described the flight of two birds in the autumn sky, and he was pleased with it.

He dared not show it to the Master, but one evening he sang it outside the hut, and the Master listened attentively but said no word.

He simply played softly on his lute and at once the air grew cool and twilight fell suddenly, a sharp wind arose although it was midsummer.

Through the sky, which grew gray, flew two herons in majestic migration, and everything was so much more beautiful and perfect than in the pupil's verses. Han grew sad and silent and felt that he was worthless.

And this is what the old man did each time. Within a year, Han almost completely mastered the playing of the lute, but the art of poetry seemed to him ever more difficult and sublime.

Near the end of two years, Han felt a devouring homesickness for his family, his native city, and his bride, and he asked the Master to let him leave.

The Master smiled and nodded. "You are free," he said, "and may go where you like. You may return, you may stay away, just as it suits you."

So Han went off his journey and traveled uninterruptedly until one morning in the half light of dawn he stood on the bank of his native river and looked across the arched bridge to his home city.

He entered secretly into his father's garden and listened through the window of the bedchamber to his father's breathing as he slept.

Then he slipped into the orchard beside his bride's house and climbed a pear tree, and from there he saw his bride standing in her room combing her hair.

And while he compared all these things which he was seeing with his eyes to the mental pictures he had painted of them in his homesickness, it became clear to him that he was, after all, destined to be a poet.

He saw that in poets' dreams reside a beauty and enchantment that one seeks in vain in the things of the real world.

Han climbed down from the tree and fled out of the garden and over the bridge, away from his native city, and returned to the high mountain valley.

There, as before, sat the old Master in front of his hut on his modest mat, striking the lute with his fingers. Instead of a greeting he recited two verses about the blessings of art, and at their depth and harmony the young man's eyes filled with tears.

Once more Han stayed with the Master of the Perfect Word, who, now that his pupil had mastered the lute, instructed him in the zither, and the months melted away like snow before the west wind.

Twice more it happened that he was overcome by homesickness. On one occasion, he ran away secretly at night, but before he reached the last bend in the valley the night wind blew across the zither hanging at the door of the hut, and the notes flew after him and called him back so that he couldn't resist them.

On the second occasion, he dreamed he was planting a young tree in his garden, and his wife and children were gathered around him and were watering the tree with wine and milk.

When he woke up, the moon was shining into his room. He got up, disturbed in mind, and saw in the next room the Master lying asleep with his gray beard; trembling gently.

He was overcome by a bitter hatred for this man who, it seemed to him, had destroyed his life and cheated him of his future.

He was about to throw himself upon the Master and murder him when the ancient opened his eyes and smiled a sad but sweet and gentle smile that disarmed his pupil.

"Remember, Han Fook," the aged man said softly, "you are free to do what you like. You may go to your home and plant trees, you may hate me and kill me, it makes very little difference."

"Oh, how could I hate you?" the poet cried, deeply moved. "That would be like hating heaven itself." And he stayed and learned to play the zither, and after that the flute.

Later on, he began, under his Master's guidance, to make poems and he slowly learned the secret art of apparently saying only simple and homely things but thereby stirring the listener's soul like wind on the surface of the water.

He described the coming of the sun, how it hesitates on the mountain's rim, and the noiseless darting of the fish when they flee like shadows under the water, and the swaying of a young birch tree in the spring wind.

When people listened, it was not only the sun and the play of the fish and the whispering of the birch tree, but it seemed as though heaven and earth each time chimed together for an instant in perfect harmony. Each listener was impelled to think with joy and pain about what he loved or hated, the boy about sport, the youth about his beloved, and the old man about death.

Han no longer knew how many years he had spent with the Master beside the source of the Great River; often it seemed to him as though he had entered this valley only the evening before and been received by the old man playing on his stringed instrument.

Often, it seemed as though all the ages and epochs of man had vanished behind him and become unreal.

Then one morning he awoke alone in the house, and although he searched everywhere and called, the Master had disappeared.

Overnight it seemed suddenly to have become autumn, a raw wind tugged at the old hut, and over the ridge of the mountain great flights of migratory birds were moving, though it was not yet the season.

Han took the little lute with him and descended to his native province. When he came among men they greeted him with the salutation appropriate to the aged and distinguished.

When he came to his home city he found that his father, his bride-to-be and his relations had all died and other people were living in their houses.

In the evening, however, the festival of the lanterns was celebrated on the river and the poet Han Fook stood on the far side of the darker bank, leaning against the trunk of an ancient tree.

When he played on the little lute, the women began to sigh and looked into the night, enchanted and overwhelmed, and the young men called for the lute player, whom they could not find anywhere, and they exclaimed that none of them had ever heard such tones from a lute.

But Han Fook only smiled. He looked into the river, where the mirrored images of the thousand lamps floated. Just as he could no longer distinguish between the reflections and reality, so he found in his soul no difference between this festival and that first one when he stood there as a youth and heard the words of the strange Master.

Hermann Hesse

Augustus

Elisabeth's husband died shortly after their marriage leaving her poor, young and pregnant. She felt utterly abandoned as she sat alone in her little apartment waiting to give birth to a fatherless child.

Elisabeth thought constantly of her expected child and daydreamed about the many beautiful, splendid things she wished for the little one.

A stone house with plate-glass windows and a fountain in the garden was one of the many wishes. As for his career, she wished he would become a college professor or a physician.

Binswanger, an aging man with silver hair lived next door to Elisabeth. He seldom went out and would often go unseen by anyone for long periods of time.

When he did get out, he used to put on a wool hat and carry a green umbrella. Children used to get frightened of him and grown-ups whispered that he probably had good reason to live such a retired life.

Sometimes in the evening a delicate music, from a harpsichord, would drift out of the window of his small apartment. Passing children would ask their mothers whether angels were singing inside and their mothers would answer that it was probably some kind of a music box.

Elisabeth and Binswanger had an odd kind of friendship, they hardly spoke to each other, but Binswanger used to tip his hat or take a friendly bow every time he passed Elisabeth and she used to nod gratefully in return.

Elisabeth kind of liked the little gray old man and used to think to herself that if things should ever go bad for her she would definitely ask him for help.

In the evening, as Elisabeth sat alone gazing darkly through her window feeling sorry for herself as she remembered her dead husband or worried about her child's future, soft comforting music would flow from Binswanger's window like moonlight through silver clouds.

Binswanger had several old geranium plants growing outside his window that he always forgot to water, but they were always green and full of blossoms and never showed a wilted leaf because Elisabeth used to water and take care of them.

One raw and windy late autumn evening, Elisabeth realized that her hour had come and felt frightened because she was entirely alone. As night fell, an old woman with a lantern in her hand knocked on her door. When she entered the house, she boiled water, laid out fresh linens and did everything that is needed to be done when a child is about to be born.

Elisabeth allowed herself to be looked after in silence and only when the baby was there, wrapped in fine new baby clothes and in deep sleep, did she ask the old woman who she was. "Binswanger sent me," the woman said, and the weary mother fell asleep.

When Elisabeth woke up the next morning, she found her son sleeping besides her and breakfast, with freshly boiled milk, ready for her. Everything in the room was neatly arranged but the old woman was gone.

When the baby woke up and started screaming because he was hungry, Elisabeth took him to her breast and felt happy to see him healthy and handsome. Then she remembered his father, who did not live to see him, and tears welled up in her eyes.

She hugged the little orphan child and smiled once more, then fell asleep with the little one in her arms. When she woke up, there was a freshly cooked soup, more milk, and the child was wrapped in clean linens. Elisabeth was back on her feet in no time, healthy and strong again, and could take care of herself and of little Augustus.

When Elisabeth realized that her son need to be baptized and that she had no godfather for him she thought of Binswanger. One evening, as twilight fell and the sweet music was pouring out of the little house next door once more, she went over to Binswanger's place.

She knocked timidly on the door and was greeted by a cordial: "Come in!", and the music stopped. There was a little old table in the middle of the room with a lamp and a book on it and everything was neat.

"I came to thank you for sending me that good woman. I intend to pay her as soon as I can work again and earn some money." said Elizabeth, "But now I have another worry." she continued, "Little Augustus need to be baptized but I have no godfather for him."

"Yes, I thought of that too," said her neighbor, stroking his gray beard. "It would be a good thing if he were to have a kind, rich godfather who could look after him if things should ever go badly for you. But I too am lonesome and old and have few friends and so I cannot recommend anyone to you, except, perhaps, myself, if you would accept me."

This made the poor mother happy, and she thanked the old man and enthusiastically agreed. The following Sunday they carried the baby to the church and had him baptized.

The same old woman appeared there too and gave the child a silver coin. When Elisabeth objected, the old woman said:

"Take it. I am old and have what I need. Perhaps this coin will bring him luck. I was glad for once to do a favor for Binswanger. We are old friends."

They went back to Elisabeth's room together and she made coffee for her guests. Binswanger brought a cake, so it turned into a real baptismal feast. After they had finished eating and drinking and the infant had long since fallen asleep, the old man said diffidently:

"Now that I am little Augustus's godfather, I would like to present him with a king's palace and a sackful of gold pieces, but those are things I do not have. I can only add another silver coin to the one from our neighbor.

However, what I can do for him shall be done. Elisabeth, you have certainly wished your little boy all sorts of fine and beautiful things. Now think carefully what seems to you to be the best wish for him, and I will see to it that it comes true.

You have one wish for your youngster, whatever one you like, but only one. Consider well, and this evening when you hear my little music box playing, you must whisper your wish into your little one's left ear, then it will be fulfilled."

Then he hastily took his departure and the neighbor woman went away with him, leaving Elisabeth dumbfounded, and if the silver coins had not been there in the crib and the cake on the table, she would have thought it all a dream.

She sat down beside the cradle and rocked her child while she meditated and considered many beautiful wishes. At first she planned to make him rich, then handsome, then tremendously strong, then shrewd and clever, but at each choice she felt some hesitation, and finally she concluded that all this was really only the old man's joke.

It had already grown dark and she had almost fallen asleep sitting beside the cradle, for she was weary from playing hostess, from her troubles and from thinking of so many wishes, when suddenly there drifted over from next door a faint, subtle music, more beautiful and delicate than had ever been heard from a music box.

At the sound Elisabeth gave a start and remembered, and now she once more believed in her neighbor and in his gift as godfather, but the more she reflected and the more she wanted to make a wish, the more confused her mind became, so that she could not decide upon anything.

She was greatly distressed and had tears in her eyes, then the music sounded softer and fainter, and she knew that if she did not make a wish that very instant, it would be too late. She sighed aloud and bent over her boy and whispered in his left ear: "My little son, I wish for you — I wish for you —" and as the beautiful music became fainter and fainter, she was frightened and said quickly: — "I wish for you that everyone will love you."

The music had now completely died away and it was deathly still in the dark room. She bent over the cradle and wept and was filled with anxiety and fear, and she cried: "Oh, now that I have wished for you the best thing I knew, perhaps, it was not the right thing. And if everyone, every single person, loves you, still no one will ever love you as much as your mother does."

Augustus grew up to be a handsome boy with bright vibrant eyes. He was spoiled by his mother and well liked by everyone. Elisabeth quickly realized that her wish for her child was coming true, for the little one was hardly old enough to walk on the streets when everyone he met found him so pretty and clever that they patted his hand and openly admired him.

Young mothers smiled at him, old women gave him apples, and if at any time he was naughty, no one believed that he could have done wrong; or if it was obvious that he had, people shrugged their shoulders and said: "You really can't hold anything against that dear little fellow."

People who had noticed the handsome boy came to see his mother, and she who had once been so alone and had very little sewing work to do, now as the mother of Augustus had more patrons than she could ever have wished.

Things went well with her and with the youngster too, and whenever they went out walking together, the neighbors smiled and turned to look after the lucky boy.

The best happened to Augustus next door at his godfather's, who would sometimes call him over to his house in the evening when it was dark and the only light in the room was the little red fire burning in the black hollow of the fireplace.

The old man would sit the child beside him on a fur rug on the floor and would tell him stories as they both stared at the quiet flames.

Occasionally, when a story was ending and the little boy became sleepy staring with half-open eyes at the fire in the dark silence, then out of the darkness flowed sweet music, and when the two had listened to it for a long time in silence, it often happened that the whole room was suddenly filled with tiny sparkling angels who flew in circles on bright golden wings, dancing elaborately around one another in pairs and singing at the same time.

The whole room resounded in a harmony of joy and serene beauty. It was the loveliest thing Augustus had ever experienced, and when later on he thought of his childhood, it was the dark, quiet room of his old godfather and the red flames in the fireplace and the music and the festive, golden, magic flight of the angelic beings that filled his memory and made him homesick.

As the boy grew older, there were times when his mother was sad and felt compelled to think back to that baptismal night. Augustus ran merrily about in the nearby streets and was welcome everywhere.

People gave him nuts and pears, cookies and toys, all kinds of good things to eat and drink, set him on their knees, let him pick flowers in their gardens, and often he did not get home until late in the evening and would angrily push aside his mother's soup. If she then was unhappy and wept, he would look bored and go sullenly to his cot. If she scolded or punished him, he screamed and loudly complained that everyone except his mother was nice and kind to him.

She was often seriously angry at her son at these troubled times, but later, as he lay sleeping among his pillows and the light of her candle shimmered in his innocent childish face, then all harshness left her heart, and she would kiss him cautiously so as not to awaken him.

It was her fault that everyone loved Augustus, and sometimes she thought with sorrow and almost with dread that perhaps it would have been better if she had never made that wish.

Once she was standing beside Binswanger's geranium window, cutting the withered leaves from the plants with a pair of scissors, when she heard the voice of her son in the courtyard that lay behind the two houses, and turned around to look for him.

He was leaning against the wall with a disdainful look on his pretty face, and in front of him stood a girl taller than he was, saying coaxingly: "Come now, you'll be nice, won't you, and give me a kiss?"

"I don't want to," Augustus said, putting his hands in his pockets.

"Oh, please do," she said again. "I'll give you something nice."

"What will you give me?" the boy asked.

"I have two apples," she said timidly.

"I don't want any apples," he said contemptuously and started to leave. But the girl caught hold of his arm and said cajolingly: "Wait, I have a beautiful ring too."

"Let's see it!" Augustus said. The girl showed him her ring, he looked at it carefully then took it off her finger and put it on his own, held it up to the light and nodded approvingly.

"All right then, you can have a kiss," he said carelessly, and gave the girl a hasty peck on the mouth.

"You'll come and play with me now, won't you?" she said confidently, taking his arm. But he pushed her aside and shouted rudely: "Leave me in peace, can't you? I have others to play with."

The girl began to cry and ran out of the courtyard. He looked after her with a bored and exasperated expression, then he turned the ring around on his finger and examined it. He began to whistle and walked slowly away.

His mother stood still with her garden scissors in her hand, shocked at the harshness and contempt with which her child had treated another's love. She turned away from the flowers and shook her head and said over and over to herself: "Why, he's bad, he has no heart at all"

When Augustus came home a short time later, she took him to task, but he looked at her laughingly with his blue eyes and showed no sign of guilt. Then he began to sing and he was so affectionate with her, so funny and charming and tender, that she had to laugh, and she decided that with children one shouldn't take everything so seriously.

But the youngster did not entirely escape punishment for his misdeeds. His godfather Binswanger was the only one for whom Augustus felt any regard, and in the evening when he went to see him his godfather would say: "Today no fire is burning on the fireplace and there is no music, the little angel children are sad because you were so bad."

The boy would go home in silence and throw himself on his bed and weep, and for many days afterwards he would try hard to be good and kind. Nevertheless, the fireplace burned less and less often and his godfather wouldn't be bribed with tears or hugs.

By the time Augustus was twelve years old, the enchanting angelic flight in his godfather's room became a distant dream, and if by chance he did actually dream about it in the night, then on the following day he would be doubly wild and boisterous and order his many friends about with the ruthlessness of a field marshal.

His mother had long since grown tired of hearing from everyone how fine and charming her boy was, she had nothing but trouble with him. When one day his teacher came to her and said he knew of someone willing to enter her son in a distant school, she went next door and had a talk with her neighbour.

Soon thereafter on a spring morning a carriage drew up and Augustus in a fine new suit got in and said farewell to his mother and his godfather and all the neighbours because he was to travel to the capital and study there. His mother neatly parted his hair for the last time and gave him her blessing. The horses moved off and Augustus rode away into the big world.

Many years later, when Augustus became a college student and wore a red cap and a moustache, he traveled back once more by carriage to his home town because his godfather had written that his mother was very ill and could not live long.

The youth arrived in the evening, and people were amazed to see him get out of the carriage followed by the coachman, who carried a big leather trunk into the house.

Elisabeth lay dying in the old low-ceiling room. When the handsome student saw her looking white and withered on the white pillows, only able to greet him with her quiet eyes, he sank down weeping by the bed and kissed her chill hands. He knelt beside her the whole night through, until her hands grew cold and her eyes lifeless.

After his mother was buried, Binswanger took him by the arm and led him into his little house, which seemed to the young man shabbier and darker than before.

They sat together for a long time with only the small window shimmering feebly in the darkness. Then the old man stroked his gray beard with his thin fingers and said to Augustus: "I will make a fire in the fireplace, then we won't need the lamp. I know you must leave tomorrow, and now that your mother is dead, you won't be back again very soon.

Binswanger kindled a small fire in the fireplace, pulled his chair near it, and arranged Augustus's chair close to his own.

They sat together for another long while, looking into the glowing coals, until the flying sparks had grown sparse, and then the old man said softly:

"Farewell, Augustus, I wish you well. You had a fine mother who did more for you than you know." His godfather said.

"I would have gladly played music for you again and shown you the small blessed ones but you know that isn't possible any more.", he continued. "You must not forget them and you must remember that they always continue to sing and that perhaps you will be able to hear them once more if a time comes when you desire it with a lonely and longing heart. Now give me your hand, my boy, I am old and must go to bed."

Augustus shook hands with him but could not speak. He went sadly over to the deserted little house and for the last time lay down to sleep in his old home, but before falling asleep he thought he heard again, very far off and faint, the sweet music of his childhood.

He left the following morning and nothing was heard of him, in his home town, for a long time. He soon forgot his Godfather Binswanger and the angels.

Augustus lived a life of luxury and revelled in it. No one could equal his style as he rode through the streets waving to adoring girls and teasing them with secret glances, no one could drive a four horse carriage with such elegance, no one was as cheerful and animated during summer night's drinking bouts in the garden.

He took a rich widow for a lover. She gave him money, clothes and horses; everything he needed or wanted. He traveled with her to Paris and to Rome and slept in her silk sheets.

His beloved, however, was the soft, blonde daughter of a burgher; he met her recklessly in her father's garden, and she wrote him long, ardent letters when he was abroad. But the time came when he did not return.

He found friends in Paris, and because his rich mistress began to bore him and study had long since become a nuisance, he stayed abroad and lived the life of high society.

He kept horses, dogs, women, lost money and won money in great golden rolls, and everywhere people pursued him, were captivated by him and served him, and he smiled and accepted it all, just as hc had accepted the young girl's ring long before.

The magic of his mother's wish lay in his eyes and on his lips, women smothered him with tenderness, friends raved about him, and no one saw that his heart had grown empty and greedy and that his soul was sick and full of pain.

At times he grew tired of being loved so by everyone and went alone in disguise to foreign cities, but everywhere he found people silly and all too easy to conquer. Everywhere he scorned the love that followed him so ardently and was content with so little.

He often felt disgust for men and women because they did not have more pride, and he spent whole days alone with his dogs in a beautiful hunting preserves in the mountains. A stag stalked and shot made him happier than the conquest of a beautiful spoiled woman.

Then in the course of a sea voyage he chanced to meet the young wife of an ambassador, a reserved, slender lady of the northern nobility who stood out with marked distinction among the many fashionable women and worldly men.

She was proud and quiet, as though no one was her equal. As he watched her, he noticed that her glance seemed to brush past him too hastily and indifferently. It seemed to him as though he was experiencing what love is, for the very first time. He determined to win her heart.

From then on, at every hour of the day, he stayed close to her and in her sight. Since he was always surrounded by people who admired him and sought his company, he and the beautiful unmoved lady were always at the centre of the company of travelers, like a prince with his princess. Even her husband treated him with deference and went out of his way to please him.

It was never possible for him to be alone with the lovely stranger until, in a southern port when the whole party of travelers left the ship in order to spend a few hours sightseeing, he managed to remain by her side. Soon, in the colourful confusion of a market-place, he managed to engage her in a conversation.

He led her into one of the many small dark alleys leaving the square, she followed him trustfully but when she suddenly found herself alone with him she became nervous and looked around for their traveling companions.

He turned to her passionately, took her reluctant hand in his, and begged her to leave the ship with him and flee. The young woman grew pale and kept her eyes fixed on the ground.

"Oh, that is not knightly," she said softly. "Allow me to forget what you have just said."

"I am no knight," cried Augustus. "I am a lover, and a lover knows nothing except the one he loves and has no thought except to be with her. Flee with me, we will be happy."

She looked at him solemnly and reproachfully with clear blue eyes. "How could you know that I loved you?" she whispered sadly, "I cannot deny it; I love you and I have often wished that you might be my husband. For you are the first I have ever loved with all my heart. Alas, how can love go so far astray!

I would never have thought it possible for me to love a man who is not pure and good. But I prefer a thousand times to stay with my husband, whom I do not greatly love but who is a knight full of honor and chivalry, qualities that are foreign to you.

Now, do not say another word but take me back to the ship; otherwise, I will call out to strangers to protect me against your disrespectful behavior."

No matter how much he stormed and pleaded, she turned away from him and would have walked on alone if he had not silently gone after her and accompanied her to the ship. There he had his trunk taken ashore without saying good-bye to anyone.

From then on, the luck of this much-loved man changed. Virtue and honor had become hateful to him, he trod them underfoot and diverted himself by seducing virtuous women through his magical wiles and exploiting unsuspecting men whom he quickly made his friends and then contemptuously cast off.

He reduced women and girls to poverty and forthwith disowned them, he sought out youths from noble houses whom he seduced and corrupted. There was no pleasure that he did not indulge in and exhaust, no vice that he did not cultivate and then discard.

There was no longer any joy in his heart, and to the love that greeted him everywhere no echo responded in his soul.

Sullen and morose, he lived in a magnificent country house on the seacoast and tormented the men and women who visited him with the wildest whims and spitefulness.

He took delight in degrading people and treating them with complete contempt; he was satiated and disgusted with the unsought, unwanted, undeserved love that surrounded him.

He felt the worthlessness of a squandered and disordered life in which he had never given but always simply taken. Sometimes he went hungry for a long time just to be able to feel a real appetite again, to satisfy a desire.

The news spread among his friends that he was ill and needed peace and solitude. Letters came but he never read them, and worried people inquired of his servants about his state of health.

He sat alone and deeply troubled in his house by the sea, his life lay empty and desolate before him, as barren and devoid of love as the billowing gray salt sea. His face was hideous as he huddled there in his chair at the high window, holding an accounting with himself.

White gulls swept by on the coast wind, he followed them with eyes empty of all joy and sympathy. As he reached the conclusion of his meditations and summoned his valet, only his lips moved in a harsh and evil smile.

He ordered that all his friends be invited to a feast on a given day, but his intention was to terrify and mock them on their arrival with the sight of an empty house and his own corpse. For he was determined to end his life by poison.

On the evening before the appointed feast he sent his whole staff of servants from the house, and the great rooms fell completely silent. He withdrew to his bedroom, where he mixed a powerful poison in a glass of Cyprus wine and raised it to his lips.

As he was about to drink, there was a knocking at the door, and when he did not reply, the door opened and a little old man entered. He went straight up to Augustus and carefully took the full glass out of his hands, and a familiar voice said: "Good evening, Augustus, how are things going with you?"

Astounded, angered, but also ashamed, Augustus smiled mockingly and said: " Binswanger, are you still alive? It has been a long time, and you actually do not seem to have grown any older. But at the moment you are disturbing me, my dear fellow.

I am tired and was just about to take a sleeping potion."

"So I see," his godfather replied calmly. "You are going to take a sleeping potion and you are right, this is the last wine that can still help you. But before that we'll chat for a minute my boy, and since I have a long journey behind me, you won't mind if I refresh myself with a small drink."

He took the glass and raised it to his lips and, before Augustus could restrain him, tilted it up and drained it in a single gulp. Augustus became deathly pale. He sprang towards his godfather, shook him by the shoulders, and cried sharply: "Old man, do you know what you have just drunk?"

Binswanger nodded his clever gray head and smiled. "It's Cyprus wine, I see, and it's not bad. You don't seem to be in want. But I haven't much time and I won't detain you for long if you will just listen to me."

Disconcerted, Augustus stared into his godfather's bright eyes with horror, expecting to see him collapse at any instant. But Binswanger simply sat down comfortably on a chair and nodded benignly at his young friend.

"Are you worried that this drink of wine might hurt me? Just relax. It's nice of you to be worried about me. I would never have expected it. But now let's talk again as we used to in the old days. It seems to me that you have become satiated with a life of frivolity? I can understand that, and when I leave, you can refill your glass and drink it down. But before that I must tell you something."

Augustus leaned against the wall and listened to the little old man's good kind voice, a voice so familiar to him from childhood that it awoke echoes of the past in his soul. Deep shame and sorrow overcame him as he looked back at his own innocent youth.

"I have drunk your poison because I am the one who is responsible for your misery. At your christening your mother made a wish for you and I fulfilled it for her, even though it was a foolish wish.

There is no need for you to be told what it was; it has become a curse, as you yourself have realized. I am sorry it turned out this way, and it would certainly make me happy if I could live to see you sitting beside me once more, at home in front of the fireplace, listening to the little angels singing.

That is not easy, and at the moment it might seem to you impossible, that your heart could ever again be healthy and pure and cheerful. But it is possible, and I want to beg you to try.

Your poor mother's wish did not suit you well, Augustus. How would it be now if you allowed me to fulfil a wish for you too, any wish? Very likely you will not want money or possessions or power or the love of women, of which you have had enough.

Think carefully, and if you believe you know a magic spell that could make your wasted life fairer and better, that could make you happy once more, then wish it for yourself."

Augustus sat deep in thought and was silent, but he was too exhausted and hopeless. After a while he said: "I thank you, Godfather Binswanger, but I believe there is no comb that can smooth out the tangles of my life. It is better for me to do what I was planning to do when you came in. But I thank you, nevertheless, for coming."

"Yes," said the aged man thoughtfully, "I can imagine that this is not easy for you. But perhaps you can take thought once more, Augustus, perhaps you will realize what is now principally lacking, or perhaps you can remember those times when your mother was still alive and when you occasionally came to see me in the evening. After all, you were sometimes happy, were you not?"

"Yes, in those days," Augustus said, nodding, and the image of his radiant youth looked back at him from afar, palely as though out of an antique mirror. "But that cannot come again. I cannot wish to be a child once more. Why, then it would begin all over again!"

"No, you are quite right, that would make no sense. But think once more of the time when we were together back at home, and of the poor girl whom you used to visit at night in her father's garden when you were at college, and think too of the beautiful blonde with whom you once traveled on a ship at sea, and think of all the moments when you have ever been happy and when life seemed to you good and precious. Perhaps you can recognize what made you happy at those times and can wish for it. Do so for my sake, my boy!"

Augustus closed his eyes and looked back over his life as one looks back from a dark corridor towards a distant point of light, and he saw again how everything was bright and beautiful around him and then became dimmer and dimmer until he stood now in complete darkness, and nothing could any longer cheer him.

The more he thought back and remembered, the more beautiful and lovable and desirable seemed that little glowing light. Finally he recognized it and tears started from his eyes.

"I will try," he said to his godfather. "Take away the old magic which has not helped me and give me instead the ability to love people!"

Weeping, he knelt before his old friend and as he sank down he felt his love for this aged man burning within him and struggling for expression in forgotten words and gestures.

His godfather, that tiny man, took him up in his arms, carried him to the bed and laid him down, and stroked his hair and feverish brow.

"That is good," he whispered to him softly. "That is good, my child, all will be well." Suddenly, Augustus felt himself overwhelmed by a crushing weariness, as though he had aged many years in an instant. He fell into a deep sleep, and the old man went silently out of the empty house.

Augustus was awakened by a wild uproar resounding through the house. When he got up and opened his bedroom door he found the hall and all the rooms filled with the friends who had come to his party and found the place deserted. They were angry and disappointed.

When he went towards them, intending to win them all back as usual with a smile and a joke, he suddenly realized that the power to do this has left him.

They barely caught sight of him when they all began to scream at him. He smiled helplessly and stretched out appealing hands in self-defence, but they fell upon him raging.

"You cheat," one man cried. "Where is the money you owe me?"

"And the horse I loaned you?" Another man added.

"Everybody knows my secrets now because you've talked about me everywhere. Oh, how I hate you, you monster!" A beautiful furious woman shrieked.

"You know what you have made of me, you fiend, you corrupter of youth!" A hollow-eyed young man with face distorted with hatred retorted.

It went on. Each one heaping insults and curses on him, all of them justified. Some hit him and several broke mirrors as they left or took valuables away with them.

Augustus got up from the floor, beaten and humiliated. When he entered his bedroom and looked in the mirror while washing, his face peered out at him, wrinkled and ugly, the eyes red and watering, and blood was dripping from his forehead.

"That's my reward," he said to himself, as he rinsed the blood from his face, and hardly had he had time to reflect a little when uproar broke out once more in the house and a crowd came storming up the stairway: moneylenders to whom he had mortgaged his house; a husband whose wife he had seduced; fathers whose sons he had tempted into vice and misery; maids and menservants he had dismissed, policemen and lawyers.

An hour later he sat handcuffed in a patrol wagon on his way to jail. Behind him the crowd shouted and sang mocking songs, and a street hoodlum threw a handful of filth through the window into the prisoner's face.

The city echoed with the shameful deeds of this man whom so many knew and loved. There was no sin he was not accused of and none that he denied. People he had long since forgotten stood before the judges and accused him of things he had done years before: servants he had rewarded and who had robbed him revealed his secret vices, every face was full of loathing and hatred.

There was no one to speak in his defence, to praise him, to exonerate him, to recall any good thing about him. He did not protest against any of this but allowed himself to be led into a cell and out of it again and before the judges and witnesses.

He looked with amazement and sorrow out of sick eyes at the many evil, angry, hate-filled faces, and in each he saw under the hatred and distortion a hidden charm and felt a spark of affection.

All these people had once loved him, and he had loved none of them; now he begged their forgiveness and sought to remember something good about each one of them. In the end he was sent to prison, and no one ventured to visit him.

In his feverish dreams he talked to his mother and to his first beloved, to his Godfather Binswanger and the northern lady on the ship, and when he awoke and sat lonely and abandoned through the fearful days, he suffered all the pains of longing and isolation and he yearned for the sight of people as he had never yearned for any pleasure or possession.

When he was released from prison, he was sick and old and no one any longer recognized him. The world went its way; people rode in carriages and on horsebacks and walked the streets; fruits and flowers, toys and newspapers were offered for sale; but no one turned to speak to Augustus.

Beautiful women whom he had once held in his arms in an atmosphere of music and champagne went by in their chauffeured horse drawn carriages, and the dust of their passing settled over him.

The dreadful emptiness and loneliness that once stifled him in the midst of luxury started to disappear. When he paused in the shadow of a gateway to take shelter for a moment from the heat of the sun, or when he begged a drink of water in the courtyard of some modest dwelling, he was amazed at how sullen and ill-tempered people treated him, the same people who had earlier responded to his proud and indifferent words gratefully and with sparkling eyes.

Nevertheless, he was delighted and touched and moved by the sight of everyone, he loved the children he saw at play and going to school, and he loved the old people sitting on benches in front of their little houses, warming their withered hands in the sun.

If he saw some young man following a girl with yearning glances or a worker returning on a holiday eve and picking up his children in his arms, or a fashionable doctor driving by in silence and haste, intent upon his patients, or a scantily dressed working girl leaning on a lamp-post, ready to offer even him, the outcast, her love, then all these were his brothers and sisters.

Each one was stamped with the memory of a beloved mother and some finer background, or the secret sign of a higher and nobler destiny.

Each one was dear and remarkable in his eyes and gave him food for thought. He considered that no one was worse than himself and decided to wander through the world and look for a place where he could be of some service to people and thus show them his love.

He needed to get used to the fact that his appearance no longer made anyone happy; his cheeks had fallen in, his clothes and shoes were those of a beggar, even his voice and gait had none of the engaging quality that had once cheered and delighted others.

Children feared him because of his scraggly, long grey beard, the well-dressed shunned his company because he made them feel soiled and infected, and the poor distrusted him as a stranger who might try to snatch away their few morsels of food.

It was hard for him to be of service to anyone. But he learned, and he allowed nothing to offend him.

He helped a little child stretching out his hand for the latch of a shop which he could not reach.

Sometimes there would be someone even worse off than himself, a lame man or a blind man whom he could assist and cheer a little along his road.

When he could not do that, he cheerfully gave what

little he had, a bright encouraging glance and a brotherly greeting, a look of understanding and sympathy.

He learned in his wanderings to tell from people's expressions what they expected of him, what would give them pleasure: for one, a loud cheerful greeting; for another, a quiet glance; or when someone wanted to be left alone, to be undisturbed.

He was amazed each day at how much misery there was in the world and how content people could be nevertheless, and it was splendid and heartening to him always to find every sorrow followed by laughter, next to each death knell a child's song, next to every greed and baseness an act of courtesy, a joke, a comforting word, a smile.

To him, human life seemed marvelously well arranged. If he turned a corner and a horde of schoolboys came bounding towards him, he saw how courage and living joy and the beauty of youth shone in all their eyes, and if they teased him and tormented him a little, that was not so bad it was even understandable.

When he caught sight of himself in a store window or the pool of a drinking fountain, he saw that he was very wrinkled and shabby. No, for him it could no longer be a question of pleasing people or wielding power, he had enough of that.

It was enlightening to see how others struggled along those same paths he had once followed and believed they were making progress, and how everyone pursued his goal so eagerly and with so much vigor and pride and joy. In his eyes, this was a wonderful drama.

Winter came, followed by Spring, then summer once more, and Augustus lay ill for a long time in a charity hospital, and here he enjoyed, silently and thankfully, the pleasure of seeing wretched folk clinging tenaciously to life and triumphing over death.

It was marvelous to see the patience in the faces of those gravely ill, and in the eyes of convalescents the increasing bright joy of life, and beautiful too were the calm, dignified faces of the dead, and fairer than all these were the love and patience of the pretty, immaculate nurses.

This period too came to an end, the autumn wind blew, and Augustus wandered forth in the face of winter. A strange impatience took possession of him, now that he saw how infinitely slow his progress was, for he still wanted to visit all sorts of places and to look into so many, many people's eyes.

His hair had turned gray and his eyes smiled weakly behind red inflamed lids. Gradually his memory too grew clouded so that it seemed to him as though he had never seen the world other than it was on that day. But he was content with it and found it altogether splendid and deserving of love.

At the beginning of winter, he came to a city. Snow was drifting through the dark streets, and a few belated street urchins threw snowballs at the wanderer, but otherwise an evening hush hung over everything.

Augustus was feeling very weary when he came to a narrow street that seemed familiar, and then another as well. And there he was standing in front of his mother's house and that of his Godfather Binswanger, both of them small and shabby in the cold driving snow but his godfather's window was bright shimmering red and friendly in the winter night.

Augustus went in and knocked at the living-room door. The little old man came to meet him and led him silently into the room, where it was warm and quiet, with a bright little fire burning in the fireplace.

"Are you hungry?" his godfather asked. Augustus was not hungry, he only smiled and shook his head.

"You must be tired," his godfather said as he spread his old fur rug on the floor. The two men huddled close to each other and gazed into the fire.

"You have come a long way," his godfather said.

"Oh, it was beautiful. I'm just tired now. May I sleep here? I will leave tomorrow."

"Of course you may. Would you like to see the angels dance once more?"

"The angels? Oh, yes, that's something I would dearly love. If only I could be a child again."

"We haven't seen each other in a long time," his godfather went on. "You have become so good-looking, your eyes are again as kind and gentle as they were in the old times when your mother was still alive. It was good of you to visit me."

The wanderer sat in his torn clothes quietly beside his friend. He had never before been so weary, and the pleasant warmth and the glow of the fire made his head swim so that he could no longer distinguish clearly between that day and earlier times.

"Godfather, I've been naughty again and Mother cried at home. You must talk to her and tell her I'm going to be good from now on. Will you?" he said.

"I will," his godfather said. "Don't worry, she loves you."

The fire burned down. Augustus continued staring into the dim redness with large sleepy eyes as he used to do during his childhood years.

His godfather took his head in his lap, a delicate eerie music drifted softly and enchantingly through the darkened room, and a thousand pairs of tiny glittering spirits hovered and circled happily about one another in elaborate arabesque in the air.

Augustus watched and listened and opened wide all his child's receptive sense to this regained paradise. Once it seemed to him that his mother called, but he was too weary, and after all his godfather did promise to speak to her.

When he fell asleep, his godfather folded his hands and sat listening beside the silenced heart until complete darkness filled the room.

57251616R00072

Made in the USA
Columbia, SC
07 May 2019